en Changeling Ten Changeling Ten Changeling

CW00660786

White Shroud

by Antanas Škėma

translated by Karla Gruodis

Vagabond Voices
Glasgow

First published in 1958 as *Balta drobulė* © the heirs of Antanas Škėma

Translation copyright © Vagabond Voices 2018

This edition published in March 2018 by
Vagabond Voices Publishing Ltd.,
Glasgow,
Scotland

ISBN 978-1-908251-84-8

Printed and bound in Poland

Cover design by Mark Mechan

Typeset by Park Productions

The publisher acknowledges subsidy towards
this publication from Creative Scotland

ALBA | CHRUTHACHAIL

The publisher acknowledges subsidy
towards the translation from the
Lithuanian Culture Institute

For further information on Vagabond Voices, see the website,
www.vagabondvoices.co.uk

Contents

Introduction

Ask any well-read Lithuanian who completed high school after 2002 which work of literature they remember best from their studies and you are almost guaranteed to hear, "Antanas Škėma's *White Shroud* – that's my favourite novel!" Lots of smoking, whisky-fuelled madness, surreal childhood experiences, unbridled passion, the essential moments of twentieth-century Lithuanian history, and plenty of displacement and alienation – all of this, combined with the author's film-worthy biography, make it understandable that Škėma enjoys cult status in his homeland. Published for the first time in Lithuania in 1988, *White Shroud* is universally viewed by Lithuanian critics as a novel that would have found its place in the Western literary avant-garde if it had been written in, or translated into, English. Recent reception of the German translation (*Das weiße Leintuch*, trans. Claudia Sinnig, Guggolz, 2017) indicates that this is finally happening: the novel was a sensation at the Leipzig Book Fair, with influential critics in the main newspapers and magazines expressing shock that Germany had not known about this work and hailing *White Shroud* as an undisputed European literary classic.

A natural *enfant terrible* and an iconoclast in Lithuanian cultural circles, Škėma felt completely at home within the broader landscape of Western literature. And the connections, influences and allusions were many. Škėma's early dramas contain echoes of Oscar Wilde's stylistic intonations, his later ones, themes similar to those of Sartre and Arthur Koestler, while his final, darkest plays have strong links to Samuel Beckett, Jean Genet and

Edward Albee. As a prose writer, Škėma was influenced by the German interwar expressionists, by Joycean stream-of-consciousness, as well as the surrealist imagery of Jean Cocteau, Henri Michaux, André Breton and Isaac Babel. Škėma's later writing has connections to Louis-Ferdinand Céline's *Voyage au bout de la nuit* and Jean-Paul Sartre's *La nausée*; the satirical New Yorkish tone of his works links him to Nathanael West. But Škėma is "genetically" closest to Franz Kafka and Albert Camus, from whom he borrowed the idea of metaphysical absurdity and the existentialist interpretation of the myth of Sisyphus, while his interest in sexuality and the dark side of human nature can be seen as inherited from Sigmund Freud.

Although Škėma's generally conservative émigré countrymen sometimes criticised him for being too heavily influenced by this broad context, he did not see this as a problem and adhered to T.S. Eliot's view that "a historical sense [...] makes a writer most acutely conscious of his place in time, of his contemporaneity." Škėma's characters do not mention big cultural names lightly. Rather, they identify with the great writers, and even the "proclaimer of the truth" himself, Jesus Christ, and without regard to epoch or language. As Škėma said in an interview, "Borrowing the notion that 'ideas float about in the air,' I think, no – I maintain that it is not you who chooses them, but they that pierce you like the arrows did Saint Sebastian, and you are then left to react to the arrows with your paper images. This is one of many means we have to prove our humanity." In reference to the question of subject matter, Škėma has said that there are thousands of subjects, but it is most important that their exploration correspond to the spirit of the "nightmarish times" in which we live. He demanded that all literature be "of its time" and felt strongly that he and other writers should not become stagnant or stereotypical.

The upheavals and catastrophes of the twentieth century, which left individuals in the Western world stranded in a harsh universe without the cover of any illusions, accompanied Škėma from the beginning of his life.

Given the many dramatic elements in both Škėma's life and work, it is fitting that he has two birth dates: his real one on 29 November 1910 and an official one, in 1911. As Škėma explains in his autobiography, he was born twice because his father wanted to trick the Lithuanian bureaucracy into providing an extra year of child benefits. Škėma was born in Łódź, Poland, where his father had been sent to work as a teacher, since, according to tsarist regulations (Lithuania belonged to the Russian Empire at the time), Lithuanian intellectuals did not have the right to work in their native country. With the start of World War I, the Škėma family retreated to Voronezh, Russia, and then spent the years immediately after the 1917 Russian Revolution in Ukraine. This period embedded in young, sensitive Škėma's memory horrifying experiences of games played with torches circling around hanged White Guardsmen, stealing potatoes, malnutrition that later caused half of his teeth to fall out, and drunken Red Army soldiers' attempts to rape his mother and shoot his father.

After many hardships, Škėma and his family succeeded in escaping from Bolshevik-held territory and returned to now independent Lithuania in 1921. However, his mother did not survive these horrors and was committed to a psychiatric hospital, where she eventually died.

Škėma made his literary debut in 1929, while living in the interwar capital Kaunas, with the novella *Fear*. Trying to be practical, he opted to study medicine instead of literature, but quickly found that the sciences did not suit his artistic temperament. With his characteristic irony, Škėma later said, "All I took from my medical studies was a love of corpses," and wrote in a letter to his close friend the Lithuanian anthropologist Marija Gimbutas that he saw writing as similar to using a scalpel. Nor did later studies in law suit the young Škėma, so he ended up supporting himself by playing cards and pool, and even marching in funeral processions. Škėma discovered himself in theatre: he began theatre studies in 1936 and later worked in theatres in both Kaunas and Vilnius. In 1938 he married Janina Solkevičiutė, who was devoted to him and greatly supportive of his work; their daughter Kristina was born in 1940.

The first Soviet occupation (1940–1941) caught Škėma in Vilnius, and he soon discovered that Bolshevism was not a joke. He received warnings while editing a satirical newspaper and later witnessed some theatre workers being arrested backstage in the middle of a performance. He later wrote ironically that this moment confirmed his beliefs about the "parallels between the tragic and the grotesque".

After this incident Škėma withdrew to the Kaunas region where, in June 1941, as the German front was approaching Lithuania, he participated in an uprising of Lithuanian volunteer fighters against the Soviet Army. During the Nazi occupation of Lithuania (1941–1944), Škėma lived and worked in Vilnius as an actor and director, and tried his hand as a playwright (his 1943 drama *Juliana* was included in the main theatre's repertoire, but the Nazi authorities banned it as too formalist). As the Germans began to retreat and Soviet reoccupation of Lithuania became imminent, Škėma realised that he would be again in danger of repressions, possibly even deportation to Siberia, and that he would never have creative freedom under that regime. Along with tens of thousands of members of the Lithuanian intellectual, business and political classes, Škėma and his family decided to flee, but upon reaching the German border he was faced with a painful choice when he was invited to join the anti-Soviet resistance. Škėma declined and the family continued to Germany, but he would always feel ashamed of his decision and controversially held that the refugees were second-rate heroes.

In Germany, the Škėmas lived in various Displaced Persons camps where refugees from across Eastern Europe endured pathetic conditions in rough barracks, cohabited with several families to a room, had no means of employment and were forced to live on meagre handouts. At first the refugees maintained illusory hopes about Allied assistance in chasing the Bolsheviks from Lithuania and they recreated organisations that had existed in Lithuania, including writers' groups (approximately seventy per cent of Lithuania's Writers' Union members ended up in the DP camps). While some of the refugees fell into so-called "DP apathy", the more ambitious, especially the younger among them, used this time more productively – they threw themselves into studies and became better acquainted with Western cultural innovations.

The DP period was a crucial one in Škėma's intellectual and creative development: he travelled with Lithuanian theatre troupes, studied translated world literature in German magazines, and spent time with other writers, eventually concentrating his energy on writing and publishing his first book of prose, *Cinders and Sparks* (*Nuod guliai ir kibirkštys*, 1947), an exploration of his painful wartime experiences. Although critical reactions were reserved, it was noted that Škėma knew how to concentrate a great deal of meaning into a single detail, as in this episode describing the bombing of a shelter: "Brain matter flew out of the split skull and splattered an edition of World History. It looked as though a mischievous boy had turned over his plate of porridge."

After four years, Škėma and his young family emigrated to the United States and settled in Brooklyn. Škėma quickly joined the Lithuanian émigré cultural scene, directing and acting in theatre productions in the US and Canada, and writing for the cultural press. Avant-garde film-maker Jonas Mekas, who was then a budding writer, remembers how Škėma was embraced by the younger generation of émigré artists and writers even though he was a decade older. In the US, Škėma was unsuccessful in finding work that even remotely suited his artistic talents, leaving him to work in a factory packing boxes and later as an elevator operator in the upmarket Statler Hotel in Manhattan where, he ironically noted, his acting experience came in handy. Škėma devoted every spare minute to his writing, even while at work.

In 1949, Škėma began to write his most important play, *The Awakening* (*Pabudimas*, published in 1956), in which he explores the nature of the Soviet regime through the challenges faced by two former classmates and the woman they both love in an NKVD (Soviet Interior Ministry) prison during the first Soviet occupation of Lithuania.

While writing *The Awakening*, Škėma was also experimenting with prose, trying out various stylistic registers. *Saint Inga* (*Šventoji Inga*, published in Chicago in 1952) contained the key story "Sunny Days" (*Saulėtos dienos*), based on true events from Škėma's early life in Ukraine. But the author's goal was aesthetics, not autobiography – to present a reverse version of the myth of a lost paradise, to express a disharmonious world view and a loss of faith in the search for any kind of harmony in the irrationality of the twentieth century. It is in this work that Škėma discovers the motif of rising and falling, which will appear in later works as Sisyphus's struggle up the mountain or as a parallel to Jacob's climbing up to Heaven. Not surprisingly, Škėma's book shocked the generally conservative, Catholic Lithuanian émigré reading public, in particular the book's transgression of sexual taboos, so that publishers forced the author to wait six or nine years for his later books to come out.

Nor did Škėma's most important work, unquestionably the novel *White Shroud* (written in 1952–54, but published only in 1958, in London), avoid angry reactions – some members of the book club that published it even cancelled their subscriptions. The scandal did not subside with the author's death: a Catholic philosopher warned the Lithuanian nation that society must defend itself from the poison of nihilism Škėma had left out for it during a difficult time.

Time has shown that, half a century later, *White Shroud* has become not only a very important Lithuanian novel, but also an enduringly popular one. The once shocking love scenes now seem quite tame, the humour and irony haven't lost their bite, the agitated, fragmentary narrative reflects the pulse of today's world, and the mass migrations of the early twentieth century offer new possibilities for identifying with the protagonist, Antanas Garšva. *White Shroud* does not present any moralising truth and refuses to explain the meaning of life, which makes it appealing to readers of different generations, especially youth.

White Shroud can be seen as a three-storey building constructed of several types of fragments. The present time of the novel, the ground floor, depicts less than twenty-four hours in the life of Garšva, a poor immigrant, once a well-known poet, who now works as an elevator operator in a large New York hotel. The second floor consists of memoir-like passages titled "From Antanas Garšva's Notebooks" which relate key experiences in Garšva's childhood and youth, and several years in DP camps; this layer is complemented by third-person accounts of traumatic episodes from his life in Lithuania, which the character himself can no longer remember. The third floor contains recent events from Garšva's life in the United States, including his love affair with the married fellow-émigré Elena, and several meetings with his friend Doctor Ignas.

The brilliance of the novel lies in how, like Joyce and Woolf, Škėma presents these narratives from different perspectives, resulting in a multi-voiced, stylistically and linguistically complex Modernist symphony. In the present time of the novel, passages of introspection shift to descriptions in an objective narrator's voice, while internal monologue is interrupted by dialogue between Garšva and hotel guests or employees. These passages of dialogue could have originally been written in English but Škėma expresses them in Lithuanian peppered with comical émigré jargon. The immigrant's daily struggle to adapt to a harsh new world is in sharp contrast to the protagonist's rich inner discourse, where he improvises on a combination of personal experiences and the great historical themes, drawing in myriad cultural allusions, literary quotes and fragments of virtually abstract Lithuanian polyphonic folk song. As he travels endlessly up and down in his elevator, Garšva is writing a poem in his head – using imagery from ancient Baltic mythology, the rhythms of atonal music, and the forms of folk wood sculpture. The reconstruction of an archaic world through poetic language is Garšva's final illusion. But as Yeats said of life in modern times, "the centre cannot hold." By the end of the novel, Garšva has not been able to write down his poem or put the fragments of his life back together in any kind of a rational structure. The grammatical and linguistic disarray of the final pages mirrors the final unravelling of his mind.

Most of the novel was written in Montreal, where Škėma went in 1953 to be with his lover, the poet Birutė Pukelevičiūte, leaving his wife and daughter in Brooklyn. Pukelevičiūte had admired Škėma's genius from the time of the DP camps and had had similar difficult experiences – in Gdansk (Danzig), Poland at the end of the war, she barely escaped the mass rapes of German women by Soviet soldiers (Škėma's mother was similarly lucky while living in Ukraine), and during the sixties she was accused of indecency for her erotic poetry. This short union was fruitful for Škėma on the creative front. Without a Canadian work permit, he was free to devote all of his time to his art – rehearsals for a production of his play The Awakening and the writing of The Elevator, as this novel was originally called.

White Shroud is Škėma's most autobiographical work. Specific events (described in some of Škėma's non-fiction texts) from the author's childhood can be found in the "notebook" entries about Garšva's mother and father. The killing of a young Russian soldier in Chapter 6 echoes an episode from Škėma's participation in the resistance to the Soviet Army. While the conflict with the patriotic DP camp poet Vaidilionis and the confrontation with an NKVD officer during the first Soviet occupation were events the author did not experience personally but was certainly very close to, the author was of course intimately familiar with and spent a great deal of time analysing the impressive hotel at the core the novel, and its complex, central symbol.

While Škėma did not inherit his mother's mental illness, he possessed some of her sensitivity and anxiety – the kind, he once joked, that "was typical of plants that have been transplanted by an amateur gardener." But as world-renowned Lithuanian-American poet Tomas Venclova suggests, "Garšva's illness is a metaphor for the whole world, which the Second World War and its totalitarian regimes threw out of kilter. It is a sick world, one in which a normal person appears ill."

Although *White Shroud* was the first work by Škėma to be published in his homeland, his writing was known by anyone who took literature seriously thanks to the steady stream of émigré fiction, poetry and criticism smuggled into Lithuania under Soviet censorship. As Venclova, who lived in Lithuania until 1977, has said, Škėma's work was a revelation and had a profound impact on the development of Lithuanian prose both within and outside the country.

White Shroud was followed by another important prose work, *Izaokas* (Isaac, first published in a three-volume anthology of Škėma's writing in 1985), which opens up a painful wound in Lithuanian history: the participation of ethnic Lithuanians in the killing of Jews during the Nazi occupation of the country. Drawing on a real historical event, the Lietūkis Garage Massacre in Kaunas on 27 June 1941 (which the author probably either witnessed or heard first-hand accounts of), Škėma probes the existence of one of the killers in post-war America, raising fundamental questions about the executioner's and the victim's roles in history, and humankind's innate sadomasochistic tendencies.

Although Škėma began his writing career believing in "man's power to survive even in the most appalling situations", by the end of his life Škėma had lost much of this faith:

> Creative nihilism is my religion. The moment of death is the most meaningful reality. And the tangle of illusions we cling to while alive. We die and others are born, live, and die. I admit that I may be wrong. And my world view is the vision of an exhausted man. But it is real.

Škėma died in 1961 in an automobile accident while returning to Brooklyn from an annual gathering of Lithuanian liberal intellectuals where he had been celebrated by friends and colleagues – one of his plays was staged, and his fiftieth birthday and the twenty-fifth anniversary of his creative career were marked. His friends felt that his death was the most refined and absurd manifestation of fate, chance, or a prank of the gods. In 1964, the émigré poet Algimantas Mackus wrote a book of poems dedicated to Škėma called *Chapel B* (after the chapel in which Škėma was laid out) and later that year also died in a car accident. These were strange coincidences with the similar death of the French existentialist philosopher and writer Albert Camus, whose ideas had had a great influence on Škėma's writing.

Decades later, Škėma's death has become a kind of legend and the writer himself a symbol of freedom and rebellion. His work gains new existential and aesthetic meaning with each epoch. During the years when Lithuania was regaining independence, *White Shroud* was especially important for its harsh, evocative depiction of the Soviet occupation and how it damaged those who remained in Lithuania as well as the refugees who were forced to retreat. The massive wave of economic emigration that Lithuania has experienced since it regained independence (500,000 people have left the country since the 1990s) highlights the conflict between individual aspiration and the need to make a living that often leads to the tragic but conscious choice of becoming a "cog in a wheel", like Antanas Garšva.

"I should have listened to a well-known Vilnius clairvoyant's advice and learned English," Škėma once said, and indeed it seemed fated that he would have trouble with that language. For decades after his death, *White Shroud* failed to appear in English, despite several translators' attempts. This task would require a translator with a particular combination of qualities – not only an excellent command of both languages, poetic intuition, and the requisite academic training, but also some of Škėma's (whose friends called him "the opposite of an archivist of traditional values") courage and innovation. *White Shroud* found such a translator in Karla Gruodis, a daughter of the DP generation, who grew up in Montreal, where most of the novel was written.

Remembering America's inhospitality towards Škėma's work, one last coincidence is worth noting. The first Lithuanian edition of *White Shroud* was published in London, in 1958; now, seventy years later, it makes its English-language debut thanks to the determination of another UK publisher.

Loreta Mačianskaitė, Institute of Lithuanian
Literature and Folklore
Vilnius, January 2018

White Shroud

White Shroud

Blessed are the idiots,
for they are the happiest
people on Earth.
The greatest wisdom is
childish; the greatest
eloquence, a stutter.

Lao Tze

The organist from Lapés
stuttered when speaking,
but he sang beautifully.

Folk saying

Prologue

BMT Broadway Line. The express arrives. Antanas Garšva steps on to the platform. Six minutes to four in the afternoon. He strides along the half-empty platform. Two black women in green dresses observe people exiting the train. Garšva zips up his plaid jacket. It is August in New York, but his fingers and toes are cold. He climbs the stairs. His freshly shined loafers shine, and there's a gold ring on the little finger of his right hand – a gift from his mother, a memento of his grandmother. Engraved on the ring: 1864, the year of the Uprising.[1] A fair-haired nobleman knelt gallantly at a woman's feet: "I may die, esteemed lady, and if I perish, my last words will be – I love thee, forgive my boldness, I love *you...*"

Garšva continues along an underground corridor to 34th Street. Mannequins pose in the storefronts. Why not install exhibits in such windows? Say a wax Napoleon, standing at ease, his hand tucked behind his lapel, and next to him – a wax girl from the Bronx. The price of the dress – *tik* twenty-four dollars.[2] *Tik tik tik tik.* Heart beating too fast. I need to warm up my fingers and toes. It isn't good to get chilled before work. There are some pills in my pocket. Good. Most geniuses were ill. "Be glad you're neurotic."

1   The 1863–64 Uprising (or January Uprising) against Russian imperial rule in the countries of the former Polish-Lithuanian Commonwealth (Poland, Lithuania, Belarus and Ukraine). The revolt was brutally repressed – over 20,000 were executed, deported, or sent into forced labor – and was followed by a strict ban on Lithuanian publications that lasted until 1904.
2   *tik:* "just" or the sound of a clock in Lithuanian.

A book by Louis E. Bisch, MD, PhD. Two doctors in one. Because double Louis E. Bisch contends, Alexander the Great, Caesar, Napoleon, Michelangelo, Pascal, Pope, Poe, O. Henry, Walt Whitman, Molière and Stevenson were all neurasthenics. A convincing list, ending with Dr L.E. Bisch and Antanas Garšva.

And Antanas Garšva turns to the right. More stairs. Too many stairs, they're repetitive. The fall of Surrealism? So be it. I'll erect Saint Anne's Church in Washington Square (Napoleon, who wanted to transplant it to Paris, can rage), and pretty nuns will file in, yellow candles in their virginal hands.[3] In 1941 in Vilnius, Elena saw a group of nuns being deported by the Bolsheviks.[4] They were taken away in a dilapidated truck, along a poorly paved street, so the little truck shook and the upright nuns kept falling down, they weren't athletic. Guards stood in the corners, pushing away the tumbling nuns with rifle butts. They split open one nun's forehead, and the nun didn't wipe away the blood, maybe she didn't have a handkerchief.

Antanas Garšva passes through the glass doors of Gimbels department store and on to the street. He holds open a door so that a freckled young woman with obviously padded bras, sixty-seven cents a pair, can slip through. He'll stop seeing her. Elena – he'll stop seeing her. Elena, I will give

---

3   A Gothic church in the Old Town of Vilnius. Passing through Vilnius, the Emperor Napoleon is said to have been so struck by its beauty that he wanted to take it back to Paris.

4   During the first Soviet occupation of Lithuania (May 1940 to June 1941), Soviet forces organised the first deportations of Lithuanian citizens to remote parts of Siberia as part of a campaign of repressing resistance to Sovietisation policies. From June 14 to 19, 1941, 17,485 people, the majority women and children, were deported. The deportations continued after the second occupation of Lithuania in 1945 and lasted until 1953; an estimated total of 245,000 Lithuanians were deported.

you a carnelian ring and an abandoned streetcar in Queens Plaza. Elena, you will mould me a nobleman's head, it's in the cornice of a house on Pylimo Street, in Vilnius. Elena... don't make me cry.[5]

Antanas Garšva walks along 34th Street to his hotel. Here's a snack bar. 7UP, Coca-Cola, ham and cheese sandwiches; Italian with lettuce. Here's a store. Sturdy English shoes, plaid socks. Elena, I will buy you new stockings. You're a bit careless – your stockings are crooked, the seam is all twisted, take them off, take them off. I will pull the new ones on to your legs myself. Firmly. Elena, I like saying your name. To the tempo of a French waltz. Ele-na, Ele-na, Ele-na, Ele-na, Ele-na-a. A little sorrow, a little taste, esprit. Pangloss was a professor of metaphysico-theologo-cosmolonigology. Stones are required for the construction of fortresses, he proclaimed. Roads are a means of transport, proclaimed a transport minister. I need your name in order to remember you. It's all reasonable. I want to kiss you again. Reasonably. Only on the lips, *tik* on the lips. I will trace Tristan and Isolde's sword on your neck with magical chalk. I will not kiss you below the neck. *Tik tik*, just just. Thank God my fingers and toes aren't cold any more. Ele-na, Ele-na, Ele-na, Ele-na-a. And here's my hotel.

Antanas Garšva goes through the door "For employees", he waves to the watchman in the glass booth, he pulls a white card from the black board. On the card – last name, elevator operator, days, hours. Clack – the clock in the metal box punches the time. One minute after four. His heart goes *tik*, the clock goes clack. The night watchmen patrol at night, punching time, clocks hanging from their necks in leather sheaths. Slender steel rods are mounted in nooks throughout the hotel. Clack – they punch. The clock is like a whore wandering from house to house. Every two hours a night watchman is allowed to smoke a cigarette,

5   Pylimo is a street in Vilnius.

7

and the clock rests on his sagging stomach. As a Lithuanian poet writes, my castle's dead sundial sleeps on the sand.[6]

Antanas Garšva climbs down the stairs to the basement. He meets a black guy who lost his right forearm to an ice machine.

"How're you doing?" the black man asks him.

Garšva replies, "Fine, and you?"

The black guy doesn't answer and climbs the stairs. One day his arm suddenly felt very hot, it fell on to a block of ice, the hot arm must have melted the ice. This black guy is a fanatic. To sacrifice your arm for a piece of ice? A heroic gesture. He's paid a dollar fourteen an hour.

Garšva walks along the basement corridors. Tin casks line the walls. Heating pipes snake along the ceiling. You can reach them with your hand. No need. His fingers are warm now. His system has performed its own blood transfusion. Leonardo da Vinci needn't have bothered with anatomy. He should have painted another Last Supper on canvas, and the dinner wouldn't have gotten mouldy. And I shouldn't have gone to the tavern to talk with Elena's amiable husband.

Kad išmanyčiau
Pusiau dalyčiau
Žalių raštų žiurstelius.[7]

Antanas Garšva walks into the changing room area. He inhales the familiar stench. The first space he passes through contains the john. The toilets are separated only by panels, so if there's someone squatting next to you, you can see his shoes and his trousers down at his ankles. And the sinks and mirrors are right there. The hotel instructions state:

6   From a 1952 poem by Lithuanian émigré poet Henrikas Nagys
     (1920–1996).
7   Lithuanian folk-song fragment:
     If I knew how
     Then I would halve
     Green patterned smocks.

employees must be clean, their hair smoothly groomed. Unruly poetic locks are forbidden. As are yellow socks and smoking in areas frequented by hotel guests. I remember the old chaplain's words, when we were children: "Now here's an example for you. Now look at this lovely child – so nice, so pretty, so clean." Oh how we loathed that teacher's pet!

"What're you so sad for today, Tony?" asks Joe, another elevator operator. A stocky, ruddy fellow. He's sitting on the bench, leafing through the *Faust* libretto. He's learning to sing baritone.

Antanas Garšva belts out, "*Aš turiu apleisti jauuu*… That's how Valentin's aria begins in Lithuanian."[8]

"What a musical language," says Joe.

"Look at me, now I'm an ambassador for the Lithuanian nation," Garšva reflects.

To the right, a doorway, and beyond it the green lockers. Antanas Garšva unlocks his locker and unzips his plaid jacket. He undresses slowly. For a while he's alone. If Vilnius didn't exist, Elena wouldn't talk about it. If a woman were not hanging on a wall (holding a violin like a prayer book, her hair loose and blue), I wouldn't talk about her. And I wouldn't hear the legend of the harpsichord or be interrogated by the judges. *Ein alltaeglicher Vorgang, A hat mit B aus H ein wichtiges Geschaeft abzuschliessan*… and so on, like in Kafka's story. A triangle: wife, lover, husband. A Lithuanian actor waved his little hand and said, "You Buridan's ass: I am the lover!" What's wrong with me today? One scene after another. Should I take a pill? Today is Sunday, today is a difficult workday.

Antanas Garšva takes out his elevator operator's uniform. Blue trousers with red piping, a beet-coloured jacket with blue lapels, "gold" buttons, braided epaulettes. Shiny numbers on the corners of the lapels. An 87 on the left, an 87 on the right. If a guest is dissatisfied with an elevator operator he

---

8   "Before leaving this plaaaa…" from the opening line of Valentin's aria in Gounod's 1859 opera *Faust*.

can note the number and report him to the starter. "That 87 is a son-of-a-bitch, that 87 took me four floors too high, 87 87 87, I wasted two minutes in this box, that goddam son-of-a-bitch 87!" It's fun to berate a number. It's fun to use numbers. 24,035 deported to Siberia.[9] Fun. Forty-seven dead in an airplane crash. Fun. 7,038,456 needles sold. Fun. Tonight Mister X got lucky three times. Fun. Today Miss Y died once. Fun. Right now I'm alone and I'll take a pill and have more fun. Antanas Garšva fishes a small, long, yellow bullet from his trouser pocket and swallows it. He sits on an empty box and waits. *Tik tik, tik tik* – my heart. In my brain, in my veins, in my dreams.

> *Lineliai, liniukai*
> *Lino žiedas, ai tūto*
> *Lino žiedas, ratūto –*
> *Linoji, linoji, tūto!*
> *Lino žiedas, ai ratūto!*[10]

Doctor Ignas likes Lithuanian folk songs. He cites verses while X-raying his patients, poking them with needles, writing out prescriptions, shaking hands, "*Lino žiedas, ai ratūto*, I hope to see you looking better on Thursday." Garšva inspired this love of folk songs in the doctor during the German occupation in Kaunas.[11] Doctor Ignas even composes the occasional poem himself, while waiting for

---

9 See note 4.

10 Folk-song fragment:
Linseed darlings, linseed dears
Linseed blossom, wheeling,
Linseed blossom, spinning –
Turning, turning – wheel!
Linseed blossom, spin!

11 The German occupation of Lithuania lasted from 1941 to 1944. Kaunas is the second-largest city in Lithuania (pop. 300,000), and was the country's capital during the interwar period of independence. It is located at the confluence of the Neris and Nemunas rivers.

his patients. He consults Garšva at length about every stanza. His round little face blushes pink like a girl's when he receives a compliment. His poems are unpretentious; they're just poems for himself. Doctor Ignas doesn't publish them, but reads them to Garšva and his father who barely reads the newspapers.

Antanas Garšva saw Doctor Ignas two weeks ago. Again an X-ray of the ribs, again the heart's zigzags etched on a scrolling band, again the bare arm wrapped in rubber while the mercury rose to whichever number the blood chose, and again the eyes were examined.

"*Vai tu rugeli, vai tu siūbuonėli,*" said Doctor Ignas when the two of them were once again seated in his office, facing each other across the desk.[12] Antanas Garšva awaited the verdict. Doctor Ignas was silent. He tilted his angelic little head, his yellow hair shone atop his broad skull, two sad wrinkles ran down from the corners of his nose, and the lenses of his horn-rimmed glasses reflected Garšva's Byzantine face. Smoke rose silently from their cigarettes. The coloured pencils stuffed into an imitation baseball turned grey.

"I'm looking forward to your next poem," said Antanas Garšva. Doctor Ignas took off his horn-rimmed glasses and placed them on his prescription pad. He blinked, like a typical myopic.

"I haven't written one," he replied sadly.

"Why?"

"Could you take some time off work?" asked Doctor Ignas.

"Is it serious?" asked Garšva.

"It's not tragic, but…"

"… but, I return to the manor and meet an old woman holding two bright candles," Garšva recalled aloud. And with this silent memory returned a summer evening, a lake, yellow water lilies, cows lowing in the distance, Jonė's

12 Folk-song fragment: "Oh you, little rye, oh you, to and fro."

tanned feet in their little white shoes, and even further back, a song. An evening in a Lithuanian backwater, where the wealthiest inhabitant was the Jew Mileris, who sold sardines from Kaunas.

"Could you be more precise?"

"It isn't that tragic. Come back the day after tomorrow, I'll examine you again and I'll be more precise. If your finances are in bad shape, I can help."

Doctor Ignas's head drooped even lower over his chest.

"I'd like to work until Wednesday. It would make for a nice round pay cheque," said Garšva.

"You can try, but be sure to come back the day after tomorrow."

Garšva got up and went towards the door. At the door they shook hands.

"*Ulioj, bite, ulioj, kadigėle!*" said Garšva.[13]

"*Bičiute, bitele – kadijo!* I'll be expecting you the day after tomorrow," replied Doctor Ignas.[14]

Garšva glances at his wristwatch. Fifteen minutes to start time. Not so tragic. There are no more tragedies. The remaining New York theatres stage dramas and comedies. Tragedies are staged in museums. A plaid jacket and brown trousers hang in the locker. This elevator operator's uniform is modernised Johann Strauss. Person number 87 could get sick wearing a uniform from an operetta. I didn't go see Doctor Ignas the day after tomorrow. The next day I telephoned Elena's husband and we met in Stevens's tavern. Should I drop work, change out of my uniform, and go to see Doctor Ignas? I feel strange. The contour of the peeling cupboard door looks like a giant ear. Who banned surrealism from Lithuanian literature? Was it Mažvydas?[15]

---

13 Folk-song fragment: "Hum, bee, hum, buzzee."

14 Folk-song fragment: "Buzz, dear bee, Buzz little bee!"

15 Martynas Mažvydas was the author of the first printed book in Lithuanian, *Katekizmo prasti žodžiai* (Simple Words of the Cathechism; Königsberg, 1547).

Kaukus, Žemepatis ir Lauksargus pameskite, imkiet mane ir skaitykiet.[16] I can't take off my uniform. I'm a Lithuanian *kaukas* in a Strauss operetta. *Imkiet mane ir numarinkiet ir tatai marindami permanykiet.*[17] There are no more tragedies. There are the peeling cupboard doors, an empty Coca-Cola box, a few minutes to start time. *Tik tik, tik tik* – in my temples, in my veins, in my dreams. *Imkiet mane, bičiute, bitele, kadijo!*[18] The celluloid bullet has dissolved, the bitter powder has shrouded the brain. Number 87 already feels calmer, more fun. A chemical blanket has enveloped this number. Elena, I will not be able to give you a carnelian ring or an abandoned streetcar wagon in Queens Plaza. It doesn't matter, Elena, soon it won't matter at all.

---

16 "Give up your *kaukai*, your harvest and field gods, take me and read me instead." From the Lithuanian Preface of Mažvydas's *Catechism* (1547), the first book printed in the Lithuanian language. In it, Mažvydas addresses common Lithuanians, urging them to give up pagan beliefs and embrace Christianity, which the state officially adopted in 1387.

A *kaukas* (plural: *kaukai*) is a type of brownie or gnome in Lithuanian mythology, thought to live under a house or in the ground nearby. *Kaukai* were thought to bring good luck or *skalsa*, a type of non-material wealth associated with economy and the efficient use of resources, and they might do small, useful tasks. A Lithuanian housewife traditionally left small gifts to attract one of these positive, chthonic beings to her home, even sewing a tiny garment with a single piece of thread and hiding it in a corner. Lithuanian semiotician A.J. Greimas's analysis showed that the word *kaukas* is associated with water, dampness and earth. *Kaukai* were also associated with death, as at some points they were thought to be the spirits of stillborn children.

17 "[…] take me and read me, and in reading consider this […]", from the opening lines of the Preface to Mažvydas's *Catechism*.

18 From Mažvydas's *Catechism* and a folk song: "Take me, dear bee, buzz little bee!"

Chapter 1

Stevens's tavern is quiet during the day. Lively Bedford Avenue is around the corner, so incidental drinkers rarely stop by. Stevens's – Steponavičius's – clientele are labourers. They fill the place on evenings and weekends, and Stevens's plump and experienced face lights up with an obliging smile. His hands move instinctively, and a joke slips out instinctively, and Stevens instinctively nods his head if he has to comfort an unhappy tippler.

When Antanas Garšva entered the dark tavern at ten that morning, Stevens was reading the *Daily News*. Stevens liked this slim, slightly stooped, fair-haired man who often came in during the day. He had a nice voice, and didn't boast or complain. Stevens was happy to have a daytime customer relationship with the man. Chatting with Antanas Garšva made Stevens feel that his own life was in pretty good shape.

Antanas Garšva once again looked at the familiar objects, the familiar face. Light-coloured tables covered in reddish checked tablecloths, the floor clean for the moment, the polished and gleaming bar and mirrors, the red vinyl of the chairs, the television hanging in a corner of the ceiling. Only the old boxers' portraits looked dusty, like neglected relics.

Antanas Garšva once again noticed the slight but pervasive smell of beer and urine, heard the rustling of the *Daily News*, and said:

"Hello there, Mister Stevens!"

"Hello there, Mister Garšva!"

The bar owner's face brightened with the gentlest version of his obliging smile.

15

"A mother strangled her three-year-old child and then jumped from her fourth-floor window. It happened in the Bronx," Stevens offered pleasantly.

"Not too close to here. How about some White Horse?"

"Surely you've got some good news, if you're having scotch?" asked Stevens.

"Another customer will be coming by soon. We've got some important business to discuss."

Garšva sat down at the bar. He saw his face in the mirrors, in the convex glass of the bottles. Fair and pallid, dark rings under his eyes, and bluish lips. A reflected mask that was begging to be ripped off and discarded.

"This is a good bar, Stevens. I'd buy one like this."

"Save up, and I'll sell you it," said Stevens as he poured scotch from a gurgling bottle.

A hurried gulp and quick breathing, red circles on the cheekbones. "This guy is in bad shape," thought Stevens.

"If it goes well, I'll ask to be a partner," said Antanas Garšva. "Pour me some."

"OK. Sure…"

Squares of sunlight spread across the floor. The round lid of the jukebox glistened – a magician's crystal ball containing the tavern's warped interior and expanded perspective, the doors and street now farther away. And in this oblique instability, the furniture and the other people froze. Antanas Garšva swallowed a second mouthful. His face fogged up in the mirror and his eyes glittered. "He's overexcited; I don't like how he's rubbing his hands on the bar," Stevens observed. Outside a white mongrel loitered by the door and then ran off, its tail up. Dimes and nickels rested on the bar; change waiting to return to a pocket.

"Nice weather," Garšva said.

"Yea. Not so hot any more," agreed Stevens.

Elena's husband opened the tavern door. Wide shoulders, dark hair, blue eyes, worn grey suit, polo shirt, protruding chin, determined and sad, he looked like a lost centaur.

He lingered at the door. Garšva slid off his chair. Elena's husband waited, leaning forward somewhat, his stiff short hair aggressively erect. Garšva took a few steps. They stood facing each other until their eyes agreed they would not shake hands. "If there's a fight, Garšva's finished," Stevens decided.

"Let's sit down," said Garšva. They chose a table by the jukebox.

"What will you have?"

"What are you drinking?"

"White Horse. Can I get you one?"

"Uh-huh."

"Two," Garšva raised two fingers.

"And two glasses of seltzer."

The mongrel returned, lingered by the tavern doors and disappeared. Stevens brought over the scotch and the seltzer, and returned behind the bar to pick up his *Daily News*. For a moment, the rustling of the newspaper and Garšva's rapid breathing were the only sounds in the tavern. Elena's husband poured some scotch into his seltzer.

"I'm not trying to interfere," stressed Garšva.

"I know," replied Elena's husband.

Garšva looked up.

"Elena told me."

"She spoke about me?"

"She told me everything."

Elena's husband sipped his drink calmly.

"I was going to kill you."

"You *were* going to?"

"I was. But I changed my mind. Love is stronger than death, isn't it? You should know, you're the poet."

"This is a ridiculous situation. I asked you to come... because I hold the opposite view."

Elena's husband put his glass down on the table suddenly. Several drops of his drink fell on to the reddish tablecloth.

"Death is stronger than love," said Garšva.

17

"I'm just an engineer," said the engineer. "And I don't understand this kind of obscurity. Explain yourself."

"If there's a fight, I'll help Garšva out," Stevens decided.

"I saw my doctor yesterday."

"I know. You fainted yesterday."

"She really did tell you everything."

Garšva downed a third swig, wiped his lips with his palm. He looked at the engineer as though he were a priest giving him his penance. "I don't like to see Garšva afraid," thought Stevens angrily, opening a page of the *Daily News*. A shabby, unshaven tramp entered the tavern and asked for a glass of beer. The silence was dispersed. The whir of the distant cars on Bedford Avenue reverberated.

"I wanted Elena. She didn't agree. We talked through the whole night. Don't worry, she's faithful to you. She loves you." Garšva played with his empty whisky glass. He turned it in his fingers like a top that won't start spinning.

"I'm sorry that it happened this way," he added quietly.

"Do you love Elena?" asked the engineer, sipping his drink once again.

"Very much," Garšva confessed even more softly.

"Are you seriously ill?"

"I'm going back to the doctor. I'll find out then."

Now the engineer raised two fingers, and Stevens brought glasses of scotch and seltzer. "It looks like my guy knows how to turn a phrase. The gentleman is already giving in," thought Stevens, and he returned behind the bar to pour the dozing tramp a free glass of beer.

"What will you do?"

Garšva looked hesitantly at the full glass of scotch. He didn't have anything to play with.

"I'm not a romantic. So I won't jump from the thirty-fifth floor. I'm an aesthete, so even if I wouldn't see it myself, I wouldn't want others to see me unaesthetically crushed."

"Stop joking. What will you do?" asked the engineer, mixing his scotch into the seltzer with precision.

Garšva smoothed the tablecloth with his fingers. He focused on the beer-drinker's back, his hands and toes felt cold, and he wanted to hear Elena's voice. He knew that if he had a fourth drink he'd say something soft and helpless.

"I'm going to wait."

"Damn, why is he shaking?" Stevens got upset and poured himself some beer.

"You and I started off badly," said the engineer, watching Garšva with steady eyes. "This way we'll end up spending several hours talking without resolving anything. You have your say, and I'll go next – then we'll sum up."

"I haven't prepared a speech. Maybe I shouldn't have even asked you to come here. Elena and I had decided. I was going to ask you to divorce her. But... you know what happened. I once had to give up another woman for the same reason. I'll have to give up Elena. It will be my final retreat. We probably shouldn't have met. Forgive me. Some sort of atavistic sense of responsibility made me do it. And... I think we can take our leave now, if you have no objection."

And Garšva raised his glass.

"Put that down! Don't drink it," the engineer said sternly, and Garšva complied.

"You need help. Will you go into hospital?"

"I don't know. The doctor will decide. He just said I had to quit my job."

"Elena and I will visit you. In the hospital or at home. Send us a note."

The engineer finished Garšva's scotch, washed it down with his own, and got up. He teetered towards the bar, glanced at the slumbering tramp, and said, "Passed out first thing in the morning?"

"Just some bum," explained Stevens.

"I'll pay for everything."

The engineer returned to the table and stretched his hand out to Garšva.

"Get better. Take care. See you soon."

"Goodbye."

They shook hands. Happy to have discovered the path to the grove, the centaur thanked the slender, charming fawn. The sun's rays had now reached the bar, the bottles reflected in its mirrors glowing like ancient minarets.

The engineer let go of Garšva's hand and left. Garšva stood by the bar. "Now there's a story, and it didn't even come to a fight!" marvelled Stevens.

"Did the business go OK?" he asked.

"Yes, OK. I'm going to go now."

"Bye. Come by on Saturday. There'll be lobster. My treat."

"Thanks. Bye."

"Bye."

Garšva went out into the street and stopped, looked around for a moment. Where did the little dog disappear to, the one that had been rubbing against the door, wagging its tail?

*

Five minutes to start time. Antanas Garšva leaves the stall. He looks in the mirror. The baritone has disappeared. Mine is not a painterly face. But there are signs. Green strips along the side of the nose. But I can still move my eyes and I don't feel too bad. El Greco's cardinal has nothing on me. The red of his vestment is more dreary than my uniform's. I've cheered up, and don't care any more about the atmosphere Elena engenders. And her scent? Elena's or another woman's – in the end, what's the difference? And the swaying.

Antanas Garšva walks along the corridor to the "back" elevator. The swaying. And your acrid smell and face no longer matter. That smell that barbers get sick of: powder, hair creams, sweaty necks. You are not my beloved. You are a compliant and fetid swaying. I despise your animal magnetism. You are a shrunken anus. You are forgotten. Even though you knocked on the door and pounded it with your fists. Now you're like any other woman to me, because I am an old bachelor who chooses nutty dames rather than streetwalkers. I'm careful. Isolde? I'm just a poet. And you are material for my new poems. About Vilnius. I will write elegant legends. About Vilnius. I'll stop repeating your name. To the tempo of a French waltz. To Zola's tempo. Na na na, Na na na, Na na na, Na na naa. Elena, it's been two weeks since I had you.

Antanas Garšva is going up. The "back" elevator is packed. Black women in white smocks, Puerto Ricans with tattooed arms and the room service man with five gold stars on his uniform cuff. Every five years he's granted the honour of sewing on a star. An unnamed constellation twinkles on his green cuff. Water gurgles in the room service man's knees. When he retires, a still-spry German with two stars will jump into his place. Antanas Garšva is now upstairs. In a narrow corridor he punches another card: two minutes to start time precisely. He opens the doors.

The immensity of eight-million-strong New York fits into the main-floor lobby: an architect's model created for tourists. The mathematically designed hall – the apotheosis of reinforced concrete urban real estate – is held up by square columns, painted dark red to indicate the hotel's serious intentions, a carpet of the same colour to handle cigarette butts, armchairs upholstered in red vinyl and arranged like a waiting room for surgeries in which hundreds of doctors examine, operate, mortify. Matt bulbs shine, and tubes of "sunlight" paint visitors' faces as though they'd been resurrected from the Valley of Josaphat. A poisonously green Plymouth stands in the middle of the space – you can win it by throwing a twenty-five-cent ticket into an urn next to which sits a very cheerful young lady, groomed and coiffured like an expensive dog, her cheek muscles hurting from hours of smiling, the violet plaster of the ceiling moulding reflected in the stone on her ten-dollar ring. The blue-uniformed concierges with slicked-back hair, plucked eyebrows and a perfect ability to understand the client, walk around slavishly proud, while the black-suited manager, balding and vigilant, a regulation white carnation in his silk lapel, runs past. Tonight, a well-known band is playing at the Café Rouge, as indicated in the framed posters – stilt-like notes arranged around the French heading, around letters stencilled on to a reddish background.

On the right side of the lobby stand polished wood partitions and behind them, white-shirted – short cut, brush cut, regular cut – clerks and dark-skirted girls, endlessly accommodating to clients and furious with their neighbours, why didn't he let me use the typewriter. One thousand eight hundred and forty three hooks are installed behind a freckled clerk. That's how many rooms there are in the hotel. Nearby, in a glade of ficus and bay trees, stands a sort of pulpit that could have been ripped out of a wooden church, and a supremely elegant head concierge (grey-tufted ears, sharp nose, red bitten lips) making announcements in a muffled bass. Miss Alison is waiting for Mister Crampton, be so kind, Mister Crampton, be so kind – Miss Alison is waiting!

A row of shops stands on the left side of the lobby. The window of the first one is stuffed with souvenirs. Chinese mandarins stand side by side with Japanese geishas, painted and costumed Europeans, artificial Far Eastern characters from the immortal opera *Madama Butterfly*, clay "German" beer mugs with tangled parodies of Hals and Dürer, Dutch hats – the sighs of an Americanised Dutchman, varnished Negro masks that would make someone from the Congo or Sudan laugh Homerically, Indian-patterned tablecloths carefully woven by modern looms, countless porcelain knick-knacks. Next is a window of men's accessories. Each shirt, tie or pair of boxers embroidered with the hotel emblem: a roaring, somewhat English lion, and the hotel's name. The same lion appears next door, embroidered on the women's accessories. And the hotel's greatest source of pride – the watch display case in the centre of the lobby. Contemplating it can inspire a panicked sense of one's own commonness – a very simple, thousand-dollar watch bracelet, a fine string of pearls, mother-of-pearl earrings, small, barely visible rings studded with shimmering diamonds.

The main-floor lobby contains a drugstore that serves tasty fishcakes. And a coffee shop for the more humble clientele. The ageing waitress will be let go tomorrow; she was chewing gum on the job and the assistant manager noticed. You can also find a news and tobacco kiosk in the main-floor lobby; the bald, grey owner, a member of a sect with only eight hundred followers, plays the flute on Sundays. A few steps down, still within the main-floor lobby, is a spacious restaurant with samples of imported wine bottles arranged on a granite stand like multicoloured candles on a gigantic cake. In the main-floor lobby you can get a haircut or a shoeshine, or stop by the Ladies' or Gentlemen's and have a pleasant chat with an attractive black man or woman whose skin makes the white towels stand out. You can buy cigarettes from a girl in a low-cut dress who walks around with a tray hanging from her neck, and if you're in a rush she'll call a friend who sells herself as if it were a spring discount. Here you can complete various monetary transactions, and even go mad – an experienced doctor will rush down from the tenth floor.

The steady rhythm of the lobby is broken by the red bellhops: they attack the luggage of the arriving and departing, they chat up guests who feel like talking and are discreetly silent if a new arrival doesn't want to, and many have the psychological insight of a psychoanalyst. It's as difficult making it into the bellhops as getting into the French Academy. Unless someone retires or dies. In a week, an experienced bellhop can collect a hundred dollars in tips.

One minute to start time. Antanas Garšva walks along, observing himself in the mirrors. There's Garšva, there's

Garšva, there's Number 87. I have acquired a new coat of arms. My genealogical tree has branched out. My mother's coat of arms contains an upright fish. Some kind of carp, maybe a crucian. The roaring lion has swallowed the rotten fish. Long live the digestive capacities of foreigners. Long live paralysed England, reincarnated into a hybrid between a fish and a lion. Long live grapefruit and the fusion of hydrogen bomb elements before the explosion. Long live my break periods. The American Dream. And the fog. You can't come near me. The hotel guests, the manager, or the starter. Not even the starter. The last mirror. Look at yourself one last time, Antanas Garšva. Suddenly, perhaps accidentally, you look like your father. Company over for tea and wild strawberry jam would say: "Sooooo like your mother! Turn around, Antanukas. Look – a perfect copy!"[19] If they thrust a violin into your hands it would befit you to play Wieniawski's gypsy variations. My friend Joe, the baritone, is already waiting. And my friend Stanley, the drunk.

Antanas Garšva finds himself in a spacious sunken area of the lobby lined on two sides by elevators. Six to the left and six to the right. To the left – the locals. They go up to only the tenth floor, stopping at each one in between, and then return. To the right – the expresses. They stop once at the tenth floor and then at each one after that, up to the final, eighteenth, floor. The hotel elevators are automatic, manufactured by Westinghouse. Signalling machines mounted on the walls flash with green and red lights that track the movements of the elevators. Like at intersections. This area of the lobby is bordered by the window of the flower shop. Beyond the polished glass – roses, gladioli, rhododendron, carnations, azaleas, and white- and red-veined hothouse leaves, an anatomical atlas woven of human blood and nerves.

By the window of the flower shop, the starter is waiting for a new shift of elevator operators. A tall, bilious,

19   Antanukas is a diminutive of Antanas.

blue-uniformed Irishman, he is short-tempered and swift, and prone to sudden, inexplicable bouts of anger. He collects the cards and assigns the elevators.

"Number nine, Tony," he says, handing out a pair of white gloves. Above the elevator door – numbers and arrows. Antanas Garšva waits for his friend to descend. The arrow shows twelve, stop, down, no stop at eleven. Number nine will soon shoot down to the lobby. I have put on my surgical gloves. My grandmother's ring, from the time of the rebellion, is hidden. Dear madam, you are strange, I no longer care about Elena. I am a dreamer, just like my father. I am a Lithuanian *kaukas* in the biggest hotel in New York. Forty elevator operators alone. Number nine has flown down. The door opens. Seven passengers stream out. The short Italian says, "Today one drunken idiot stuffed a dollar into my hand. You've got your red. Goodbye, Tony."

Garšva enters the polished box. The pen, as the elevator operators call it.

Chapter 2

From Antanas Garšva's Notebooks

My father loved to play the violin. Though he had no formal training, he played with talent. He performed the Wieniawski variations furiously, but I doubt he could have handled Bayer. He would drop whole rows of notes, replacing them with brilliant improvisation. Like all amateurs, he had a tendency to stretch, emotionalise and accelerate. His attitude was that of the quintessential violinist: a thin and agile body, nervous and elegant hands, a sharp profile with a long, hooked nose. Good God, how he flew around the room! Each pose was worthy of art photography. Later, I would recognise my father in Walt Disney films, in different cartoon characters. When I first started reading serious books, I saw the image of the "genius" in my father's violin gymnastics. Listening to his infernal playing, I would feel tears of beauty well up, a longing to die in the name of the ecstasy exploding inside me.

It would happen in the evening. We had a fancy oil lamp with a green glass shade. In the evenings the lamp glowed, softening the shabby walls and furniture, making them look splendid and cosy.

As my mother embroidered and I played with my hands, my father would turn his eyes away from us and then, seemingly by chance, graze the surface of the violin hanging on the wall above our heads. He waited to be asked. The clocks ticked – our family loved clocks. The glowing wall clock, the twin bell alarm clock, my father's silver watch on the table, my mother's hanging from her neck like an enlarged medallion. We would listen to the clocks' introductory accompaniment. I would clench my fingers. My mother's stitching would slow down, the last petal of a tea rose would not be threaded into the tablecloth. The accompaniment ticked on for too long, as though the listeners had not yet settled in their seats, as though someone had coughed. My father was now tapping the surface of the violin nervously. How clearly we could hear the clocks! Flat stones falling into water, the sowing of fir needles, a pin digging into unpolished metal, the short, rhythmic steps of motherly love. And my mother would utter a few words, and my fingers would continue their squirrely gymnastics – as my father's melted into the violin's lacquered surface.

"What do you think?"

"About what?" my father would ask.

"I'm thinking about Wieniawski. Does his music really lack…"

"Are you trying to say – it doesn't have depth? Yes, that's true. But it is valuable for its tonal beauty. It is virtuoso, and I like virtuosity in violin music. For example…"

The violin was in his hands. I never managed to see it being taken down. As though it had autonomously removed itself from the wall and jumped into my father's hands.

"For example, this fragment from Concerto Number 2. In D minor. The very last moment. The gypsy variations. They're gems."

And my father would begin to hurl those gems around. The first to fall were tiny and unpolished, the pizzicati. These my father would throw from a seated position. Then came the turn of the larger, more polished stones. My father was now standing, and it seemed to me that he had not unfurled himself, but rather that the springs of the chair had hurled him into the centre of the room. Gems flew around in the green light, variation upon variation, while I bent my head down and curled up to avoid being injured by those musical gems. But nevertheless, the occasional sharp-edged stone would hit me in the spine and I would feel the thrill of a cold shiver. My father was very wealthy – he had more gems than a Nepalese maharaja. And he flew with them around the green room. And he contorted and raged. I couldn't understand why Wieniawski lacked depth. Gypsy variations? As far as I knew, gypsies were a deep people. They sat or danced by bonfires at night, they thrust knives into their enemies' bodies, and were good at stealing other people's horses. They were brave and dirty. Their women had a particular way of swaying from the waist, they read cards, and one wanted to embrace them to hear the jingling of the medallions hanging from their necks. Now my father was a gypsy, the green lamp a bonfire, my mother a gypsy queen, and I…

Black hair and black hair. A red sash, a bent waist. Glances meet, sparks like fireworks. I've always thought of Lermontov's Tamara as such a gypsy. How could a demon wear a red sash – he should be as black as insomniac fear in bed at night, and dancing doesn't suit him, but he can stand by the fire if the gypsy Tamara's medallions are jingling.

My father would end his variations on a long, fading note. It's possible that he got tired. Both he and his violin. I could clearly see the thinning varnish, the impressions from his fingers. The violin was old, it had to be hung carefully back on the wall, and the chair wouldn't slip under him on its own, so my father would collapse, the room having absorbed his musical enthusiasm. My mother could now return to her tea rose petal, I to my hands, my father to his thoughts. The conservatory… He had been poor – he was able to train as a teacher, but the Conservatory… the unfinished Wieniawski variations, wrinkles on the violin and on his face – two friends who joyfully throw their arms around each other and soon again part ways, two friends evading sadness. The green light inspires him to be exceptional, but that exceptionality lasts only a few minutes, and then all that's left is a cosy, bourgeois green lamp and a teacher's long evening. Notebooks, errors, problems – if there are so many kilometres from station A to station B, how many kilometres are there to station C? How far is it to station C where a conservatory stands, its magnificence confirmed by its marble columns?

And then my father wrote dramas. They were brutal, bloody and spectacular. He distinguished positive and negative characters by nationality. Lithuanians were honest, Poles – traitors, Russians – sadists. And the themes? The dissemination of banned Lithuanian books, an innocent girl's rape and tragic drowning in the Nemunas, gold prospecting in the Siberian taiga, and with it a rich accompaniment of folk songs, as though the hero's pure feelings were being poured into irregular antique pots.[20] In a small town whose once lively and noisy train station had been forgotten by the government, in the trade school building among tables, sled runners and benches smelling of resin, my father staged these dramas himself, dragging his adolescent students on to a wobbly stage that swayed on wooden trestles in the former second-class waiting room. Like the rest of the audience, I was stunned by the scenographic effects my father achieved with his naturalistic staging. Actors would scythe real rye (industrious pupils had stacked it into wooden blocks) and a special machine blew fluff representing snow, which would stick to the wool clothing of the people sitting in the front row (the front row contained the town dignitaries: the priest, the notary, the police chief, the deep-voiced midwife). The heroine of the work, sullied to the point of pregnancy by a Polish gentleman, would drown herself in a hole in the floor (the Nemunas), while a boy crouching there would hold up a

20   Banned books: books in the Lithuanian language and Latin alphabet were banned by tsarist authorities from 1865 to 1904. Nemunas: the Nemunas (Neman) River flows through the centre of Lithuania.

bottle of seltzer so that water could spray from the drowned girl's body. When the curtain was drawn back open, my victorious father would blow symbolic kisses in response to the audience's aesthetic tears. He could hear the midwife's piteous bass: "What a backward era!" An intonation that would introduce a note of humanity to the proceedings.

My father was an excellent public speaker. During ceremonies people would crowd around the linden trees and stone altar by the station. Flags fluttered, the trumpets in the firemen's orchestra sparkled, the drunken drummer belched, the town's worthies turned out in their blue and grey suits and their their facial muscles flexed with concern – an artificial convulsion to express the solemnity and grandeur of the moment. And plenty of the spectators were grateful: women eager to cry and children desperate for a show, something so rare in the town. Smoke rose from the monument. To make sure that the fire caught, the stationmaster had stuffed old newspapers under the kindling, and singed scraps flew over the assembled heads. The ladies wore hats in the Kaunas style, with multi-coloured, shimmering feathers, so that they looked like domesticated birds waiting for their feed. And my father's brain contained granaries of that kind of feed, so easily digested that it could bring tears to the eye, a slackening of the lower jaw, applause, envy for the last speaker and his family, and such a loud and unanimous "hurray" that the sound of its "ay" would penetrate the open windows of the train station restaurant and ping against a row of vodka shot glasses. My father's slim figure stood erect in its pre-war frock coat, like an obelisk staked into the ground. As in his dramas, the theme of his speech was the negative traits of Russians and Poles. His speech was structured like a Wieniawski gypsy variation. Here too he would use his introductory pizzicato, as though he were unprepared, as though he was just now searching for his words – and this search would sink into the listeners' souls, and the pizzicato would echo within their souls, and they would feel that the speaker had amassed within himself much great and meaningful content. The firemen's painstakingly polished trumpets, the nickel on the bicycles, the sand freshly scattered between the railway tracks, they all sparkled, as did the men's freshly shaven chins, the old women's dampening eyes and the silk lapels on my father's frock coat. His voice rose.

Trotsky and his accomplices were dining on the second floor of a hotel in Taganrog, throwing plates on to the street. The hungry crowd below caught the plates as though they were manna from heaven and licked them on the spot, their blue tongues quivering.

When they had Vilnius, the Poles would lure Lithuanian patriots into special interrogation rooms and pour water down their noses, and the patriots' stomachs would blow up like orchestra drums.[21]

My father would raise his arms. He shook his fists menacingly, his frock coat sleeves slicing through the air. He hurled lightning bolt glances. His vocal cords would tire. And then silence would descend. My ashen father would again stiffen, like a freshly painted obelisk on which the painter had missed two spots. His cheeks glowed with two red circles of excitement. The crowd roared, the ladies cried, the men's lips narrowed, the children's mouths gaped wide, some of them would even forget to wipe their runny noses. Round bluish clouds rolled towards the town of Žiežmariai. Members of the firemen's orchestra were already moistening their parched tongues, and the eyes of the black-whiskered conductor glanced at the sheet music. The poor drummer, stunned and exhausted, belched dwindling chords. He looked at his drum with horror, as though it were his own stomach. My father's knees slowly relaxed. The obelisk slumped, as though it had been sculpted of

---

21 Between the wars Vilnius was part of Poland 1920 to 1939, and Kaunas was the capital of Lithuania.

snow and coal, and was melting under a rain of emotion, or a fierce spring sun. My father knelt in the square by the station, by the smouldering altar, mystical fairy-tale smoke floated by his face, his arms spread wide.

"We ruled from sea to sea," he would assert.[22] "To sea" – these words would inflate and gently float away. My father would get up suddenly and walk briskly through the scattering crowd. A mad fray would crash against his back – children threw hats, trumpets rattled the beer glasses in the station restaurant, clouds rolled. My father walked like Icarus, as though he were about to ascend into the heavens and fly through the round clouds rolling towards Žiežmariai. At that time I still believed in my father – the flyer – and would not have been surprised had he actually started to fly, his long legs clearing the red-brick chimneys of the train station.

My father was a charming liar, while he lived with my mother. Later he would redirect his eloquence to a German-language teacher, and I no longer heard his heroic stories.

He studied in Tbilisi, at the Pedagogical Institute. He had no money, had survived on grapes and cheese. But he was elegant and did his best to wear well-cut clothes. Once, in the city gardens, during the evening promenade, the Georgian princess Chavchavadze ordered the driver of her open landau, drawn by four white-maned horses, to stop. My father was leaning against a blooming acacia tree, smoking a long, expensive cigarette. It was love at first sight. My father stepped into the landau without a word. The invitation was issued by Princess Chavchavadze's coal-black eyes, Princess Chavchavadze's rose-red lips, Princess Chavchavadze's hands, white as the snow atop Mount Kazbek. It was a re-enactment of the story of virtuous Joseph and Lady Potiphar. My father was proud and uncooperative,

22   In the fifteenth century, at the height of its power, the Grand Duchy of Lithuania stretched from the Baltic to the Black Sea.

and I can't possibly understand why. He would not go to the princess's hut, he declined the *shashlik* she offered, he refused to drink the red wine that had been buried so far underground in sheepskin bags, or to kiss even her smallest finger. He stepped out of the landau and went off down a narrow path between sharp-peaked cliffs. Below the road was a deep canyon. Princess Chavchavadze ordered her driver to return alone with the horses. When they disappeared around the turn, she leapt down into the roaring, foaming Terek River. Her body was never found. The swift waves of the Terek carried it to the Black or the Caspian Sea, I can't remember which one. Love died barely having been born, while my father continued to stand around in the city gardens during the evening promenade, leaning against an acacia tree. Promenaders pointed him out, beautiful women turned away timidly, and though some glanced at him admiringly from a distance, he was as immovable as that rock against which Prometheus was once chained.

Listening to these very interesting – especially to her – legends, my mother would occasionally spit out an ironic comment. That in the Caucasus, under the tsar, there were many impoverished princes and princesses, some of whom even worked as footmen, or waitresses in Tbilisi's cheapest restaurants, where you could order nothing but grapes and cheese. But my father didn't listen to these comments as he should have.

My father loved nature. I remember our walks along the Nemunas in Aukštoji Panemunė.[23] They were filled with obstacles. Flowers, juniper bushes, flowing water, clouds, the tangy smell of a pine forest – all of these would make him stop. And I found these static poses of my father's to be the most aesthetic ones.

My father kneels before a simple daisy and counts its petals. Like a botanist, like a man in love, like an orphan in a children's fairy tale.

---

23   A suburb of Kaunas, on the left bank of the Nemunas River.

My father stands on the bank of the Nemunas, watching it curve around Pažaislis Monastery.[24] His silhouette gives meaning to the landscape, and my imagination revives the past. Napoleon at the Berezina; Vytautas the Great watching the Battle of Žalgiris;[25] Genghis Khan on the Russian steppes; Nero reciting poetry as Rome burns; a pilgrim waiting for a boat to carry him to the other side, to a feast day at Pažaislis; someone about to commit suicide dismissing the final argument for the meaning of life.

My father lies on the grass, his eyes wandering among the clouds and the tips of the pines. He lies there a long time, chewing blades of grass, his chest rising rhythmically, the wind stirring his whiskers, and I expected him to utter momentous words, so all my fears and doubts would be dispelled.

I respected and loved my father when he was contemplating nature. I can only guess whether he loved it himself. He avoided conversations about it, and only spoke about it in fragments:

"Look, the sun, strange that there are six leaves, here in the marsh, when I was little I saw a lot of snakes, look, the cross is glimmering, let's sit a little longer."

And so I absorbed through my father the sadness that lies in nature, a feeling of alienation, a solitary silhouette; enveloped by the leaves, the trees, the water I would feel a million pinpricks, the loneliness penetrating my eyes, my mouth, my ears and skin.

Beautiful and terrifying – these are the first abstract words that took shape in my child's mind as I observed my father, now that he was calm in the countryside.

Sometimes my father would beat my mother.

*

Number nine is a good elevator. It rarely gets stuck between floors and the door opens quickly. Antanas Garšva stands to

---

24 A large Italian Baroque monastery complex on the outskirts of Kaunas.

25 A battle in 1410 during the Polish-Lithuanian-Teutonic War.

the right, facing a metal plate with buttons and signal lights. Red square lights up – get ready; green arrow lights up – pull the handle. Guests enter. The starter directs them. The hotel is packed on Sundays. The eighteenth floor contains halls for balls and receptions, whereas the mezzanine has a conference hall and party rooms. The hotel hosts wedding celebrations, Masonic lodge gatherings, foreign national holidays, dentists' conferences, young people's dances, parties for "The Ladies of Hercules", soirées for Russian Orthodox clergymen with red wine and tsarist songs, evenings for former alcoholics, events for Chiang Kai-shek officers, meetings of progressive Armenians, get-togethers for ageing boxers, dinners for the Cardinal and his retinue attended by Polish clerics, live chinchilla exhibitions... It commemorates, celebrates, assembles, dines, remembers, conspires, consults, honours, reviles...

The starter moves like an expressive dancer. "To your left – the expresses, from the tenth to the eighteenth floors, to your right – the locals, for the first to the tenth floors. Yes sir, the chinchillas are at the top, yes, madam, the Masons are on the mezzanine. Oh no, holy father, Parlour B is on the eighteenth, yes, the Masons are on the mezzanine, you are absolutely right – the chinchillas, forgive me, yes, the Cardinal and the chinchillas are on the same floor, Joe. To your left and to your right, yes, no, no, no, yes..."

And Antanas Garšva continues the ritual. The express – from the tenth to the eighteenth. Your floor, here we are, thank you, he presses the button, your floor, thank you, you're welcome, the button, thank you, here we are, thank you... The green arrow lights up, Antanas Garšva extends a white-gloved hand, all done, going up. He gives the handle a push, the doors close and the elevator rises. The numbers of the passing floors twinkle above him: 1, 2, 3, 4, 5, 6, 7, 8, 9, 10. Eleventh floor, here we are, thank you, a guest exits, hand to handle, we're going up, someone has stopped the elevator on the thirteenth, the doors open, a guest enters, your floor, here we are, the button, thank you, hand to handle, going up, 14, 15, the sixteenth, here we are, thank you, a guest exits, hand to handle, we're going up, 17, the eighteenth, here we are. All exit. Red square, green arrow, going down, the same ritual going down.

Up *ir* down, up *ir* down in this strictly defined space. This is where the new gods have put Sisyphus. These gods are more humane. Gravity no longer pulls the boulder. Sisyphus no longer needs sinewy muscles. A triumph of rhythm and counterpoint. Synthesis, harmony, up *ir* down, Antanas Garšva works elegantly. Here we are, and his teeth flash, thank you, they flash again, he extends his hand gracefully, his slim person is pleasing to the travellers. "You can always recognise a European," the pleasant old lady once said. "Europeans read books," she added with a sigh.

Chapter 3

The dimly lit reading room of the Kaunas Central Bookstore. Long, worn tables, yesterday's newspapers on yellow sticks, lithographs of Gediminas, Mindaugas and Valančius on the walls.[26] And the book section. Bookcases with their backs turned, and in the only opening between them at an unpainted table, a bespectacled clerk languished. Like wet sparrows, the regulars sat bent over their newspapers, unshaven and yawning from late morning boredom. Antanas Garšva was fourteen. He studied and lived alone in Kaunas, his father taught in the countryside. Sometimes Antanas Garšva would skip classes, pick out some books, and, holding his head in his thin hands, would wear out the elbows of his schoolboy's blazer, his young brain soaking up the letters and sentences. Book spines covered in brown fabric, books sewn into hard black cardboard. Thick books and thin books. Antanas Garšva read one of the thickest ones multiple times, so that the clerk noticed and would ask ironically, "You're not going to kill yourself, are you?" With a neophyte's passion, he copied any phrase he grasped into his schoolboy's notebook.

We are unhappy alone and unhappy as a community, married and unmarried, we are like hedgehogs huddling together to stay warm – uncomfortable when crowded, and even unhappier when separated; optimism is a bitter

---

26   Gediminas: the Grand Duke of Lithuania from 1316 to 1341. Mindaugas: the first Grand Duke and only king of Lithuania, who reigned from 1236 to 1251. Motiejus Valančius (1801–1875): a Catholic bishop and prominent nineteenth-century Lithuanian writer.

mockery of human suffering; life is evil, because life is war; the more perfect the organism, the more perfect the suffering; history's motto: *eadem sed aliter*; higher than conscious intellect is conscious or unconscious will; the body is a product of the will.

So Antanas Garšva absorbed Schopenhauer. But then heroes of thinner books jostled with the fat pessimist. A headless horseman, a halo of tomahawks glowing around his head, a mad Lady Macbeth stretching her unwashable hands towards the footlights, Gustave Aimard's *caballeros* – gracious to the end and making countless deep reverences with their feathered hats, a frozen Raskolnikov philosophising as he prepares to murder an unscrupulous old woman, Goethe's writhing homunculus, a Gogolesque devil rolling a hot, full moon over a Ukrainian village. The books' sculptural eyes peered into Garšva's soul, all the chaos contained in them covered by black outspread wings, and there were no more dusty reading room windows, and he was no longer curious about the feminine laughter coming from the second floor of Aušra High School.[27] Life is evil. This phrase seemed final, impossible to counter, just as it was impossible to breathe deeply in Lukšio Street – the suffocating herring smell from the Jewish shops, the homeless drunks' vomit on the stairs of the People's House, the permanent odour of Cracow sausage and Dutch cheese, dirty laundry and rotting leather shoes in his small room. Those nails chewed down while solving trigonometry questions. That damned avitaminosis pimple on his forehead, and how the high school girls laugh at him and won't dance. And that youthful longing for death, before life has even been tested.

Antanas Garšva was defeated by two collaborators: Schopenhauer and the bespectacled clerk with his haemorrhoidal humour: "You're not going to kill yourself?"

27 Aušra High School: the first Lithuanian high school in Kaunas, founded in 1915.

Antanas Garšva trusted them and, one fall Saturday, on his way home from school, he stopped by a small store in Lukšio Street. He asked for some rope.

"How many metres?" asked the old Jew with mercantile indifference.

"My death can be measured in metres," Garšva concluded sadly.

"Three metres, please. That should be enough," he replied.

"You're going away?" asked the Jew as he measured the rope.

"Far away," replied Garšva.

"My death is three metres long," he considered, deciding that this would be the last entry in his notebook of wise men's sayings. This one authored by him.

On Sunday he washed his feet, cleaned his teeth and set off for the village of Pajiesys with the rope stuffed into a paper bag. He would hang himself in a thicket, and his body wouldn't be found quickly. Black crows would peck out his eyes – the poor high school student would hang in a thicket and the mystery of his suicide would never be solved. He had never even been in love! But as the police investigators would conclude, a high school boy's soul can be as deep as Schopenhauer's or Dostoevsky's.

The dampness of the Pajiesys clay soaked through Garšva's shoes, and he was shivering. The bare willow branches brushed his face, and he gasped when a thicker one hit his pimple. There wasn't a single tree tall enough in this tangle of shrubbery. He saw the cold grim Nemunas and the hovels of Šančiai bowing to the grim waters. He pulled the rope from the bag, its clean whiteness in stark contrast to the landscape.

"Death is beautiful," whispered Garšva.

"Death is godlike. I'm nobler than Mucius Scaevola. Burning your hand is nothing. I am the only follower of the Stoics at the Kaunas high school for boys. Soon I will die, because this is the only way I can resist Schopenhauer's will."

Garšva finally found a sufficiently thick aspen and began tying his rope to a branch. Though he continued to shake, the aspen stood straight. And with the prepared noose hanging elegantly, Antanas Garšva knelt down by the tree.

"God, oh my God! I'm dying, I'm dying. How sad. I truly am dying."

Antanas Garšva crossed himself, stood up, and, having broken some branches, piled them below the noose. Then he stood on the unlit bonfire and put his head through the noose. All that was left was to jump to the side.

"Oh, if only this fire would burn! He would stop trembling, he would smell the smoke, his feet would warm up, just like in the heroic deaths of the early Christians. They would raise their eyes to the heavens." And Antanas Garšva looked up at the sky. The leaden cloud cover was still. Should he jump to the side? It's cold. It's cold. Have to repeat to myself that it's very cold, that I need to warm up, that there are matches in my pocket. Now he clearly felt the matchbox in his right trouser pocket. He could feel the edge of the matchbox against his thigh. And at the same time he almost lost consciousness. Fear came, and then in a mere second saved him. The power of fear almost knocked the pile of branches out from under his feet. But consciousness conquered his pounding heart. Antanas Garšva pulled his head out of the noose and jumped down. He took the matchbox out of his pocket and lit a single match. The little flame singed his fingertips. He dropped the blackened match. Mucius Scaevola, the early Christians, the Stoics, God – they all vanished. He scrambled up the hill to reach the road faster. In the little room in the People's House he rubbed his feet vigorously with a towel and, later, got under the covers, a collection of Pivoša's satires in one hand and a good long piece of Polish sausage in the other.[28] It was cosy. At one point he

---

28 "Pivoša" was the pseudonym of interwar Lithuanian satirist Augustinas Gricius (1899–1972).

remembered the noose in the thicket, but then quickly forgot it. He slept for eleven hours straight.

*

The elevator rises, the elevator falls. Clean, sensible, business-scented Masons disembark – the express also stops on the mezzanine. Four Chiang Kai-shek officers, cheekbones red from cocktails, emphatically pleasant and spry, leave the elevator on eleven. Four Polish clerics stand close together. Antanas Garšva lets them off on the top floor.

"The eighteenth," he says in Polish.

"Oh, my son!" Pleasantly surprised, one of them raises a hand, as though blessing him.

The nice old lady reads poetry. She once quoted MacNeice:

I am not yet born, o fill me
With strength against those who would freeze my
humanity, would dragoon me into a lethal automaton,
would make me a cog in a machine, a thing with
one face, a thing [...]

I can't remember any more. Thick and thin, on chalk paper and on wood, on parchment and papyrus, on clay tablets and on hieroglyphs etched with sharp stones into walls in caves. Books. I am not yet born. Have yet to write a good book. But the granny will soon die because she is already reborn. She reads post-war poetry. She doesn't work, lives off her capital, while I'm stuck being an elevator cog. My face, my white-gloved hand, my appearance, my polished speech – I'm a good cog.

Once upon a time a plant shot up, its roots wrenched from the ground, a gaudy butterfly floats above a field. Once upon a time... the *zauras's* jaws gaped, and the pen darts as it jots down a tune.[29] Once upon a time amoebas pressed together, and poets sing about love. Once upon a time the wheel of

29 *Zauras:* from *dinozauras* (dinosaur), a creature from Garšva's personal mythology.

time turned back, and I became a cog. And I wouldn't be surprised if my progeny turn into donkeys, pelargoniums and eventually stones. How unpleasant! Two stones will lie side by side, unable to chat. About Churchill's speech, Rilke's poetry, Parisian hats, how Petraitis is dishonest and how I'm honest: the stones won't talk about anything. All that will be left is the stars, the rising moon and water's atonal music.

I would like to be stone, water, moon, star. With eyes and a sense of my surroundings. But it's hard for me to become a cog in a machine, because I keep remembering Elena's fist banging on my door. I didn't let her in. I heard how she called my name and sobbed and fumed, and then slowly, pausing, went back down the stairs. And through the window I saw her walking in the street. Her face, as she glanced back up several times. And it's hard, because I still want to write. Will Elena help me write? Extreme individualism? That ancient, egotistical exploitation of one's neighbour? To be pleasured in bed and even get a few legends out of it? To orchestrate suffering and material for the sake of a decent poem?

Should I hire a servant?

He could follow me around, holding an umbrella over my head, and I would be able to observe and analyse the rain without getting wet. But I want to walk alone, bareheaded, and don't need any help. Up *ir* down, up *ir* down.[30] Old legends die hard. There's truth in Sisyphus's meaninglessness. When he falls, someone else will put their weight against the boulder.

"Nice weather today," Garšva says to the grey gentleman who has decided to go for a walk along 34th. "You can have a good meal downstairs," to the newlyweds who see only reflections of their embraces in each other's eyes. "Oh yes, Rocky Marciano is sure to win," to the former boxer who

---

30   *ir*: "and" in Lithuanian, often used here in the expression, "up *ir* down," as it is in the original.

proudly touches his broken nose. "No, madam, I am not French," to the girlish old lady.

And yet I can't forget. All my problems dissolve because I can still feel Elena's greyness. For renunciation was not dictated by boredom and fatigue.

Two people. Two stones, capable of speech and feeling.

"That is correct, sir. The chinchillas are on the eighteenth."

They squat in their little wooden cages, staring ahead innocently and soiling the straw. They're like shabby rabbits, those chinchillas. Why the hell would people skin them for fur coats?

Chapter 4

The sleek Studebaker raced along the tree-lined highway. Arched bridges flashed above their heads and the radio would fall silent for a moment, and then the singer would rage on again in metal-grinding tones. The engineer drove confidently. He slowed down just slightly at turns, the speedometer going back to seventy as the highway once again narrowed towards a patch of blue sky.

Elena sat with Garšva in the back seat. A small woman with a grey dress, greyish hair, grey eyes and the face of a Baldovinetti Madonna. The full lips, a detail the painter had added to accentuate her greyness. A cigarette smouldered between her thin fingers, an anachronism that matched the full lips. And she might have pulled her nylons on too quickly, because the right seam was twisted to the side. In front – the engineer's broad back, a monumental shelter as comfortingly solid as a marble portico, set off Elena's well-proportioned fragility. A plume of blue smoke rose from the cigarette, the grey eyes scanned Garšva with calm curiosity. The Studebaker careered down the grey highway through a current of green forest, the road a frozen canal, pieces of cloud slid across the blue sky, and the sun poked out unexpectedly, the layer of light powder on Elena's face a reflection of the greyness enveloping the car.

"Do you like nature?" she asked, a banal way to break the extended silence, then threw the cigarette butt out the window, where it flew off like a lifeless moth, and old, immortal shades quivered in this mechanical little world. A minor nymph dipped her feet in a spring as a slender faun watched her, and grey filaments of smoke crept out the half-opened windows, airing out the smoky car interior.

"I love water," said Garšva.

The highway curved as they passed by millionaire neighbourhoods. Past a Fred Astaire dance studio, puritanically trimmed parks, colonial-style villas, the odd Cadillac still in the drive, and the final flash of a red Shell sign.

"My wife doesn't like nature. She's still in love with Vilnius," the engineer hurled over his shoulder, turning up the radio. Another pop song, a hoarse mezzo-soprano begged to be embraced and moaned with deliberate sexuality.

Garšva studied Elena's hair and the sun disappeared once again, like a woman sitting in front of a child focused on his wooden blocks.

"I never lived in Vilnius. I know it only from frequent visits. But I remember one occurrence. A narrow street in the Jewish ghetto.[31] 1939. It was strange, beneath an archway connecting the low buildings, I met this nun, she was young and frightened and lost, and asked me for directions, but I wasn't sure myself. I suggested we look for the way together. We walked along, not sure what to talk about. It was summer, late morning, the low buildings looked empty. Along the way we met a street urchin but I couldn't get anything out of him, even though I gave him a few coins, and my nun smiled. I don't know how the

---

31   This refers to the traditional Jewish quarter of Vilnius in the heart of the Old Town, where Jewish life flourished from medieval times up to the Second World War. During the German occupation of Lithuania (June 1941 to January 1945), Nazi authorities established two ghettos in Vilnius: the Small Ghetto, which was located in the area referred to by Garšva and which was liquidated in 1941, and the Large Ghetto, which was liquidated in 1943.

two of us ended up somewhere near the Gates of Dawn.[32] As we parted, the nun said 'God bless you' and blushed slightly. I don't know why, but to me this searching captures the atmosphere of Vilnius. That city's essence has always eluded me. I often got lost in Vilnius."

"You should have asked the nun on a date – you might have discovered that essence," added the engineer merrily. Elena's lips quivered.

"I suspect she would have made the sign of the cross over me and that would have been the end of it," replied Garšva.

"Did you see the sculptures of dead noblemen on the cornices? On Pylimo Street?" asked Elena without looking at Garšva.

"I have a vague memory. I think I've seen them."

"They led you astray," she said and smiled to herself, as though Garšva were not there. The engineer turned back suddenly.

"What did you say?"

"Nothing much. We were just remembering Pylimo Street."

"Ah," and the engineer turned his attention back to the wheel. The tragic melody of a lost body was replaced by the mezzo-soprano's sexual moans. The forest's leafy greenness vanished. The highway cut through marshland. Small marsh lakes dotted with fishing rowboats, wooden changing cabins on the shores, fields of reeds. A great canopy of grey sky hung over the marsh, not a single patch of blue, the light of the sun seeped through the clouds with leaden indifference and a conspiracy developed inside the car. The woman's hands rested on her knees, the man's on the vinyl seat cover. And the woman began to breathe faster, and the man could hear his heart beating. The spring water froze

---

32 *Aušros Vartai* (The Gates of Dawn) a sixteenth-century Vilnius city gate and popular Catholic and Orthodox site of devotion that contains a famous icon, the Blessed Virgin Mary Mother of Mercy.

the soaking feet, and the faun had to close his eyes from the sun. Like statues nudged by ghosts, they shifted closer.

"If we're now talking about spiritual matters, I would hazard to say that details illuminate an atmosphere," said Garšva quietly, so that only Elena could hear.

"Could you tell me about the noblemen's heads?"

"One day," replied Elena softly.

"And there's the Jones Beach tower!" shouted the engineer.

A pointed, four-sided tower rose from the horizon, they stopped at the entrance to a long bridge, the engineer thrust some coins at the guard, and something unravelled inside the car as it once again rolled over the marshland drowning in small lakes. Garšva leaned forward, and Elena leaned back and faded into the corner. And this is how they drove into the parking lot, and the men got out to smoke and waited while Elena changed, and then the men squeezed inside to change, and when all three were finally in their bathing suits, they walked along the cement path, the pine-scented air caressing their liberated bodies, and Elena bent down to pick a daisy, and her husband stroked his hairy chest, and Garšva contemplated Elena in her close-fitting, greenish bathing suit. She walked indistinctly, as she did in her unpretentious grey dress. She was well proportioned to a fine perfection, as though she had been created by a female god. Her husband placed his feet with barbaric fierceness, a centaur turned man just learning to walk. And alongside walked the slim faun, like a Lehmbruck sculpture, an athlete's gait and the pliant muscles of a youth, if somewhat bent with a forty-year-old man's fatigue. Garšva.

The sun re-emerged. They passed closed swimming pools, playing fields, an Indian tent with a professional Indian (he told stories to children), and reached the wooden causeway that ran along the cafeteria building. And opposite was the undulating field of sand, like a gigantic Mongolian camp. Multicoloured umbrellas staked into the sand; thousands of sunburnt bodies in constant motion; discarded bottles shining like searchlights; a vibrating racket, as though the Mongolians had just finished an atonal hymn and separate sounds echoed with Dantesque immortality. Young lifeguards sat on high wooden thrones, sceptical wardens who waved with the plasticity of swimmers at anyone who went too far into the ocean. And the great river – the ocean – crashed in double rows of waves, foaming and snorting, giving and withdrawing its waters, and the damp sand happily sucked in its spattered offering.

Three people trudged down the beach. Someone might have noticed that the engineer rented an umbrella, that Elena and Garšva chatted as they stared at the ocean. Soon the trio disappeared. About a million New Yorkers went to Jones Beach that day.

*

I have just forty minutes to go. Then a half-hour break. I'll smoke two cigarettes. I'll have a talk with Stanley. Without white gloves. Good. A great calm has suddenly enveloped me. I'm even enjoying riding the elevator. My passengers are pleasant. This Mason with his tasteful, solid-coloured tie, it's even possible that Wieniawski's variations would bring him to tears. And if I told him about my past he might offer me a free vacation in Florida. Because back in Hanseatic Lübeck, his forefathers never struck their apprentices on the neck. This woman who has painted herself brown, with her wide red mouth, tiny African blossoms hanging from her ears, on weekends she swears she will love her husband to the grave. It doesn't matter that she looks like a vampire. Three innocent children hang on to vampire's skirt while she tells stories about good-natured elves, about the singing bone, about Jorinde and Joringel, about the sorcerer who ordered his wife to carry an egg, about Rip Van Winkle and nine-pins in the mountains, about, about, about – how difficult for the vampire! She left the little children at home for half an hour and is anxious to get back as fast

48

as possible. And here a thin little priest carries just a few tenners in his pocket. He gives his entire salary to the poor. When the priest walks along 3rd Avenue, he's swarmed by tramps, and they listen to the immortal words. About loving one's neighbour, how a camel can pass through the eye of a needle, and how Christ could feed bread and fish to multitudes. And the priest hands out dollars and quarters and dimes to the men gathered around him. Word and deed – what a wondrous synthesis the thin little priest carries within him.

A great calm has suddenly enveloped me. I understand the desert. The sands, the hermit's sackcloth, the rustling of desiccated leaves, a faded tent, oh, meditator, you will win God's grace, the Holy Spirit hovers above your head and geometric light rays pierce your heart. Ecstasy. No mind, no consciousness, no Greek ideas, no oriental fatalism. The Gnostic demiurge is thrown off, a trembling little devil, terrified and cowering. Oh Holy Spirit, there is imperceptible wisdom in your geometric light rays – they are based on the proportions of cupolas. Up *ir* down, up *ir* down. It's soothing to roll a boulder. I like meaninglessness. People get in, people get out. Is it for me to understand what makes the spokes of the universe turn?

I am a neophyte at solitude and an epigone of Christ. I remember Your outstretched hands and Lazarus's astounded face. I see the hair on Your legs, Mary Magdalene is kissing them. And I can see Your tensed muscles, feel Your nervous anger, the merchants and their wares flying off the temple steps. I understand Your subconscious intuition. You speak in parables, You know – we must seek. On the road to Calvary You had assistants: blows from sticks, blood, drunken tramps. You were helped along by Your pierced side, by the gathering darkness. Did Your Father remember You? The Capital Letters have endured – Your Name is written in Capital Letters.

My Brother, my Beloved, hear me.

My sin, my madness, my subjectivity, my cry, my vitality, my joy – *lioj ridij augo*.[33]

My Elevator – hear me.

My Childhood – hear me.

My Death – hear me.

Come to this hotel, stroke the lady's coiffured hair, wink at the manager, give the bellman a tip.

Speak out, Elevator Operator.

Say the only Word.

Because this great calm is killing me.

The New York desert is scorching me.

I will perish, submissive and terrified, clinging to the cowering demiurge.

My Christ – hear me, my Christ, I pray to You.

O felix culpa quae talem et tantum meruit habere redemptorem![34]

Zoori, zoori, lepo, leputeli, lioj, ridij, augo, is that the nightingale from Aukštoji Panemunė singing again?[35]

There is a sixteen-year-old girl who often goes up and down in my elevator, a friend of the cigarette girl's. She's direct. She likes me.

"Any big fish on the mezzanine today?" she asks.

"Oh yeah, I think so, and with bulging pockets," I reply with a friendly wink.

"Yesterday this old guy fondled me for two hours and didn't do anything. And paid twenty bucks. Embarrassed, I guess."

"You lucked out, Lily."

"It isn't always like that. A week or two ago, can't remember, I had to contort myself like a trapeze artist."

And Lily laughs. She laughs as though she were walking

---

33 Fragment of abstract Lithuanian folk song.

34 "O happy fault that earned for us so great, so glorious a Redeemer", a phrase used in the Catholic Easter Vigil Mass.

35 *Zoori*: "*zoori*" is a magic, invented word in Garšva's personal mythology.

towards a blue lake with a lover who is afraid to touch her hand.

"Good luck, Lily."

"Thanks, Tony."

Young girls don't exist for me any more. Once upon a time I left a small provincial town for a miniature city. For Kaunas. Modest girls with crimped hair, painted lips, hips raised on high heels, girls who would blush just from the warmth of liquor. I could no longer find that most pleasant folly. Walking through the marsh, past the swaying, grassy hillocks, you see an innocent tanned body across the lake – you are a fortune-teller staring into a crystal ball. I could no longer find the noble lie. In my father's stories, or children's books, or Boy Scout songs, or cheap oleographs with happy angels painted by some optimistic fool. I could no longer dream. I knew that the only way left to dream was through writing, and encrypted writing at that, so that fault-finding friends and critics wouldn't protest: "Sir! You are drifting towards sentimentalism!" I often cried if I saw a flower in bloom, moonlight playing on water, light-coloured hair tousled by a spring wind, and even a buzzing fly. Not permitted. A stern clerk sits in the centre of my brain. Sorting thoughts and feelings. The clerk has been sitting in the same chair for forty years. That is why he's so pedantic and unappeasable. No, sir, you are not allowed to be sentimental! Away with these papers – scrunch, scrunch and into the bin. They belong to the cleaning lady. He's logical, the stern clerk. If I don't listen to him, I'll lose. Like Dante and his heaven, like Dostoevsky and his whining characters.

The fortune-teller's clear ball. Hold on, Lily. Save your money. Buy yourself a little store and marry a man who drinks beer only on Sundays. Dante himself can't choose a sphere of paradise for you and Dostoevsky won't dare make you cry. Keep spinning on your trapeze.

Antanas Garšva glances at his watch. Just seventeen

minutes to go. Oh, merciful cigarette, I pray to you! My Christ, what did you feel when Mary Magdalene fell at Your feet? There was a time when I loved Jonė and thought... Does it matter what I thought? If I should go mad and start sobbing in the elevator, I doubt there would be a writer who could create a literary version of my tears. I need to swear. It helps. Goddamned sons of bitches, fucking whores, impotent losers, reeking dysenterics, syphilitic gigolos, shit-eaters, granny-necrophiliacs. What other vile things can I think up?

"Such nice weather today, madam. You look lovely! I barely recognised you," says Garšva to a sixty-year-old hotel guest.

"You're so charming," she replies. And they both smile.

Chapter 5

From Antanas Garšva's Notebooks

Women have only been episodic in my life. One hustler's words really stuck in my head: "Don't push yourself to the limit. As much fury and as little emotion as possible. The curve of your neck is childlike. Your eyes and eyelashes are feminine. You love like a man. Fight, and you will win."

And I fought. I perfected the art of love. I developed all sorts of psychochemical techniques. I blended tenderness with biting sarcasm. I would pleasantly quote a good poem and then make a snide comment about a passer-by. I measured passion consciously so that it would erupt into an unexpected storm just when my partner thought that I was completely spent. I knew how to make her think that I will be the one to break it off, so she must cherish me. I knew how to vary things – when to be sad and when to be cheery, when to be angry and when to pretend to be sorry. I succeeded in sprinkling so-called love with the sugar of friendship. So that after the breakup my lovers would go on to advertise me to others.

My women were like Matisse's Lorrain Chair, which brings out the blue monumentality of the wallpaper behind it. Loving them helped me feel the reality around me more sharply. I would suddenly perceive objects, their manifestations, which I would normally have indifferently passed by. The sky, a masonry wall, a child's fine hair, the ghostly light of street lanterns, the distant hum of train engines... and it would become clear to me: I have been given live material, I am full, and I must write, and I must leave my beloved, be alone, until everything dwindles, fades, loses all colour and relief.

I could easily tell when the end was near. Just as I fused with my beloved in a heavy, crushing embrace, that point when, as one falls into the abyss, the stems of thought shimmer with the leaves of death, at that very moment I would suddenly feel very sad. As if the last drops of love had run out. And I would feel angry: they were not intended for this woman. And I would remember Jonė. I understood in theory: I won Jonė when I gave her up. But this paradoxical consolation mocked me like a grotesque dervish mask.

About three kilometres from the small town, past the draining marshes – where storks still stepped and lapwings shrieked, where the cries of drowned maidens still echoed – there was a lake. A boring little lake surrounded by greyish hills. And when, as a nineteen-year-old stripling, I would swim to the other side, past the yellow water lilies to the muddy shore, I knew: within an hour or two Jonė will come here, and we will observe each other, and then we will go home.

We couldn't swim together. The town didn't approve of bathing suits. Men and women splashed around separately, divided by the narrow lake. They could clearly see each other's naked bodies, and on Sunday afternoons the men and the women would trade hackneyed jokes about the features of those bodies, and ringing laughter would cut through the air. Often, couples hoping to get married would initiate intimate relations with mere glances, so that, when a blushing bride walked into the church with her pallid fiancé, he was already familiar to her, and she felt safe leaning against his shoulder.

Jonė and I were there on holidays from Kaunas, we wore bathing suits, we couldn't swim side by side, the town's moral code forbade it, because Jonė was a poor girl being raised and put through school by relatives, an upstanding notary devoted to Preferans, and his upstanding wife – a dentist who didn't like doing fillings, preferring to rip teeth out without mercy.

I can still remember her distinctly, a sixteen-year-old girl always wearing some tight little garment, with kind eyes; I haven't forgotten her slim, athletic back; I still love her nervous embrace, her responsive lips, how she was impressed by my idiotic poems. Losing Jonė was losing my youth – when real life came to an end and the cautious, cunning battle with death began.

We met at the volunteer firemen's fancy-dress ball. The organisers had laced streamers in the national colours around the ceiling of the small middle school's auditorium, stringing them to a coloured lantern hanging in the centre, as though the evening were a celebration of Lithuanian-Chinese cooperation.

The masked figures loitered, not sure what to do. Zosė the servant girl, who came as a bale of hay, stood in the corner of the room, the dancers grazed the skirt she had woven for weeks, and the dried-out straw crumbled to the floor, and Zosė was furious because her impressive outfit did not attract a single partner.

The postman Zaleckis, in a devil's mask, tried to entertain the crowd from the centre of the room. He brushed the dancers' legs with the black-painted rope he had sewn to his velvet trousers, offering them private rooms in hell. But nobody laughed, and the devil eventually drank himself into a stupor in the canteen and fell asleep face down on a table, snoring loudly, his breathing obstructed by the mask.

There was also a clock with a dial painted on his behind, about six girls in Lithuanian folk costumes, an astrologist (his pointed hat promptly fell apart and lost its stars), two rabbits, one donkey, and so on.

The firemen's brass band played a *suktinis*, some waltzes and polkas, "Elytė" (the only foxtrot they knew), and the "Pantera" tango to the tempo of a funeral march.[36]

---

36 *Suktinis*: Lithuanian folk dance with pairs.

The kiosk lady sold only two rolls of streamers, and a kid who had snuck in for free stole a bag of confetti and then ripped it open right there, scattering confetti all over the floor. The most important guests neither danced nor caroused. They drank in the canteen.

I had finished high school that year and was spending the holidays at my father's. I gave the coat-check lady my white university student's cap. I walked around the hall proudly. I danced the foxtrot with a Jewish girl from Jonava. We made a date to go for a walk near the semaphore guarding the defunct train station, a spot favoured for illicit love.

Jonė had come with her cousin, the notary's son. I knew him. Jonė's boyishly cut hair was slicked back. She was wearing a high school uniform. The notary's son explained that she was going into eighth grade.[37] I asked her to dance. Her slim little body pressed against mine, our heads pressed together, I could feel her childish breasts. That was the style of dancing then. I smelled her hair and suddenly lost my nerve, slowly pushed her away from me, and started doing something strange with my feet to justify my distance. Other couples flashed by. The cymbals went crash, crash, the trumpets told their sincere lies, one of the Lithuanian sashes detached from the Chinese lantern and I pulled it down as I danced. Jonė must have noticed something in my expression.

She asked, "Are you angry?"

"Lousy band," I replied.

Later I walked her home. The notary's son had disappeared earlier, with the Jewish girl from Jonava. It was a warm summer evening, we walked along the narrow sidewalk, stepping carefully so as not to fall into the ditch that ran along it. It was a very good sidewalk. Old, worn and slippery, requiring me to grip Jonė's arm above the elbow. After all, she could have slipped, she could have fallen into the ditch.

---

37 In the Lithuanian secondary school of the time this would have been equivalent to the final year of high school.

And when we reached the notary's house with its long, open veranda we stopped, not sure what to talk about.

"Nice veranda," I commented.

"Sometimes, at night, I sit here, when I can't sleep," said Jonė.

"What do you think about?"

"I dream."

"About what?"

We were sitting on a wicker bench on the veranda. Facing us stretched an empty field, watched over by the summer moon. Like faint candles, train lights occasionally flashed in the distance across the field. The twinkling lights and fog hanging over the marsh blended with the moonlight.

Jonė didn't reply, and I knew what to do. I was only nineteen, but knew something about embraces. I even had a running list of girlfriends. Seamstresses, factory workers, prostitutes. All I had to do was reach over and touch Jonė's hair. And, if she didn't turn her head away, I would be entitled to her neck, her shoulders, her lips. Without moving my hand I asked again:

"What do you dream about?"

"Nothing. Anything. I just sit and look at the field. I like warm summer nights like this and often can't sleep."

She stirred.

"I'm going to go in," she said.

"Wait a second. Can we see each other?" It just escaped from my lips.

"I don't know. They keep an eye on me. I have to listen to them."

And she told me about her penniless father, a security guard at the Kaunas Conservatory, about her mother, soaking in a laundry, about the great fortune of having been taken into the notary's care. And she got up.

"Wait until Vytautas gets back," I said. That was the name of the notary's son.

"I'm afraid. He'll make fun of me."

And I didn't turn towards her. I got up and squeezed her small, hard hand and gave a gallant bow, as my mother had taught me. Then I turned like a soldier, stopped suddenly, turned around, and clumsily bent over to kiss Jonė's forehead. Then I jumped from the veranda on to the narrow sidewalk, so that the notary's house would recede as quickly as possible, so that I wouldn't appear confused or silly. At the corner of my own street I met the whistling notary's son.

"How was the Jewish girl?" I asked quickly.

"Tomorrow, by the semaphore. Same deal." We chuckled cynically.

The same full moon shone the next night. I sat in my room, looking through the window at the moon's craters, from where I thought poetry would wing its way down. I had decided to study literature. I wanted to write a few good poems over the summer, so I would enter university with some talent. Books lay on the table. Verlaine, Baudelaire, Poe, A Thousand and One Nights. I held a pen in my hand. I was ready to receive a moon crater muse at any moment. She would blind, pierce, reward me. A blank sheet of paper awaited. My alarm clock ticked. There were no dogs barking, no people's voices, the small town was asleep. I knew that inspiration doesn't just suddenly jump into a poet's soul. I observed the moon's craters, listened to the alarm clock, waited. But the muse wasn't inclined to visit me. I thought to myself, "If only a dog would bark, or some drunk swear out loud!" It was quiet. I got up and glanced at the mirror on the wall. "Now that's what I call a poet's face," I decided. "My long hair, my dreamy eyes. Yes, my skin is quite tanned – I could be from Brazil. Maybe I should drink wine, smoke a pipe and swear? Do I even need inspiration?" And I calmly began to write.

A good hour later I had a finished poem. It's hard to remember it accurately now. It was something about three or four hanged men swaying from bleak linden branches.

A harsh wind blew. A girl with tousled braids sobbed, her arms around the most handsome hanging man's legs. And the poet was terribly sorry, because the (two or three) others didn't have any passionately sobbing girls. At the end of the poem the moon shone, reacting to this tragedy with macabre resignation.

I straightened up victoriously. I glanced in the mirror and grinned, "Now there's a poet." But then I realised that another upper tooth had cracked. Black holes were ruining my smile. "Craters everywhere," I thought to myself. And then, as it had in Palanga, my pride wilted.[38] I reread the poem. I didn't like it any more. "Craters, craters, craters everywhere," I repeated through clenched teeth. The poets lying on this table are killing me with their perfect stanzas. And where am I supposed to find an olive tree to sit under, like Homer, making beautiful marble arrangements? I need to get out, go for a walk, that's recommended for anxious types. And I crept quietly out the door.

But as soon as my shoes began rhythmically tapping the sidewalk, I remembered Jonė. I looked at my watch. Just after twelve. Yesterday Jonė said that she often sits on the veranda daydreaming. A counterbalance to the craters! Tonight I will reach out with my hand, I will kiss Jonė's lips instead of her forehead, I will hold her tight. And no, I won't take her to the semaphore! I can sit holding her tightly much longer than I can work on my poem about the hanged men.

The veranda was empty. As was the wicker bench. And, like yesterday, the field stood bare, guarded over by the summer moon. And at the other end of the field some train lights twinkled sparsely, like faint candles, the twinkling lights and the fog on the marsh blending with the moonlight.

I waited for two or three hours. Every faint rustling, distant and obscure sound, swooping bat, a silence that was

---

38   Palanga: Lithuanian seaside resort town on the Baltic Sea.

like music, except that the notes were so high I couldn't hear them – each of these moved me, and I wanted to weep, and tried to control myself. Jonė didn't come out to dream. I went home and ripped up my poem.

The holidays were coming to an end, and I was still only walking Jonė back from the lake. We traipsed all over the marsh. I would hold her hand, but didn't dare kiss her, didn't have the nerve to ask why she didn't go out on to the veranda. And I had loitered around the notary's house for two weeks now. Each night was the same. The moon's left side slowly melted away.

And then one afternoon, as were walking back to her house, Jonė smelling of water, it just slipped out.

"You're a little liar."

"Me?" she asked, surprised.

"Yes, you. You never go out on the veranda at night. I know – I've been going over to your house. You pretend to be serious, but you're a little liar."

Jonė laughed. Her teeth were uneven, but white and shiny. She laughed for a long time, and I got angry.

"You shouldn't laugh about romance." Jonė was walking next to me, with her tanned legs, her little cloth sneakers.

"I can't sit on the veranda," she said. "I'd have to go through their rooms, and they'd wake up. I only dream about the veranda."

"You could climb out the window. You'd just need to jump down about a metre. I know."

Jonė clasped her hands behind her back, kicking clumps of earth with the heels of her shoes.

"I'll be there tonight. At exactly midnight."

Jonė glanced at me. I'm sot sure, but I may have seen fear in her eyes. When the municipal pump house came into view, we parted in silence. I stayed on the marsh and watched until Jonė's tanned legs disappeared over the bank. But for the next half-day, all I saw was their glistening muscles.

I was standing by the veranda well before midnight.

Clouds cloaked the sky. The marsh fog escaped on to the empty field and crept down the street. I could feel its damp caress. Formless bodies wrapped around my own, and when I shook my head trying to get free of them, hundreds of fingers stole under my collar in a gentle frenzy, and my skin trembled and I froze, trapped by a feeling of foreboding. It wasn't a normal trembling, as the night was warm, but an old and familiar feeling of anxious waiting loomed over me once again like a strict and concerned stepmother.

I wiped my face with my hand. Just like that time in Palanga, I wanted to cry out words, and not ones borrowed from books. This cry slithered through my consciousness like a snake. By a black sea, huge shards of rock lay on the sticky ground. Strange-shaped snails, parched crabs, rotting fish, and ferns hanging before my eyes like stiff fans.

I turned around. Jonė was waiting on the veranda. I hadn't noticed her jump out of the window. I leapt on to the veranda, grabbed Jonė's hand and pulled her on to the sidewalk. We almost ran to the train station that never saw any trains, to where the semaphore stood. I pressed myself against Jonė with the full strength of my muscles, and she yelped. I clamped myself to her lips, and at the same time my hands, harsh and tearing, threw her down on to the grass. I saw her nakedness: her hips, the dark triangle of her lower abdomen, and when I detached my lips for a second to draw some air into my lungs, I heard her sharp, deep-throated cry.

Jonė screamed, and once again I saw the black sea, and the messy piles of track links became gigantic shards of rock, and strange-shaped snails, crabs, fish and ferns were coming at us. Jonė screamed, and it was a scream that I had heard before, when I didn't have arms or legs and had rolled like a ball through the blind darkness. Jonė screamed, and my pulsating blood wanted to burst from my swollen veins. I stifled Jonė's cry with my hand. She fell silent, and I took her.

When it was all over I said, "You should get dressed."

And, as she cleaned herself up, I stared at the semaphore. At the leaning semaphore with its smashed signal lights, its post etched with swear words and hearts. And I turned back hesitantly.

"You OK?" I asked.

"You ripped my dress," replied Jonė, and she broke out in sobs.

"Let's go home. Walk next to me. I won't touch you," I uttered, staring at the ground. We went back. Gradually she stopped crying, and all I could hear was her rhythmic sniffling. We stopped at the veranda.

"Don't be mad at me," I said quietly. "Could you wait?"

"For what?" asked Jonė. And I felt relieved.

"I really love you, Jonė. Try to understand, I got carried away, one day I'll explain. Could you wait until I get settled, until I get a job? I'll never do that again. I promise."

And then, with my trembling hand I touched Jonė's hand, and she didn't pull hers away.

"I'll marry you, Jonė. OK?"

"OK," she said. And she kissed me on the cheek.

"You go to sleep now. We'll meet tomorrow, at the lake. OK?"

"OK."

And I went home. And didn't see, or feel, or hear the enveloping night.

We made love, of course. For three years. In the pine forest at Aukštoji Panemunė, under the hazelnut trees by the Jėsa, in my room, in my friend's room. And, when I started to cheat on Jonė, I continued to believe: one day I'll marry her.

A small town. A greyish lake in a ravine. The draining marsh where storks still stepped, and lapwings shrieked, and where, sometimes, you could hear the moans of drowned spirits. The old, narrow, slippery sidewalk. The masked figures, pathetic in their powerlessness. The volunteer firemen's brass band playing the "Pantera" tango at the tempo of a funeral march. The notary's veranda. The semaphore. My youth – erupting in poems of hanging and first love.

*

The three men sit on a bench in the changing room, smoking. Joe, Stanley, Garšva.

"I'm going to Philadelphia next week," says the baritone Joe.

"What for? A girl?" asks Stanley. He reeks slightly. He's had some whisky. Stanley has gone grey, even though he is only twenty-seven years old. His hands shake, he has a red nose like his grandfather, a bankrupted *šlėktelė* from Masuria.[39] He's straight and flat. He knows these words in Polish: *dziękuję, ja kocham, idz srač,* and, for some reason, *zasvistali – pojechali.*[40]

"No. The Philadelphia radio invited me. They're paying for my trip, meals and hotel, and another twenty-five dollars in my pocket."

"You'll put it in the bank, right?" Stanley asks, to confirm.

Joe's round face reddens. "Not in the liquor store's cash register, of course."

"Then what are you turning red for?"

Joe clenches his fist.

"What a load of crap," says Stanley, pulling deeply on his cigarette.

"Joe wants to sing. It isn't funny," says Garšva.

"Anyone with a gaping mouth makes me laugh," Stanley notes calmly.

"And what about you?" asks Joe.

"Me too. That's when I stick a bottle down my throat."

---

39 *Šlėktelė*: Lithuanian version of the Polish term for landed gentry (*szlachta*).

40 *Dziękuję, ja kocham, idz srač* and *zasvistali – pojechali*: Thank you, I love you, go to hell, and that which shall be shall be (Polish).

Stanley shakes the ash off his cigarette.

"My girlfriend has a really deep belly button," he says suddenly.

Garšva stares at Joe.

"In two years you'll sound like that too. Two years of working in the elevator would scramble anyone's brain."

"You won't have to wait. Your brain got scrambled when you were in your mother's womb."

"Watch it, Stanley," growls Joe.

"Nice note. B flat, I think," remarks Stanley. Joe stares, surprised. Stanley starts to whistle.

"Where's that from?" he asks.

"I dunno," replies Joe childishly.

"From Allegro assai. Mozart. The Fortieth Symphony. G minor."

Stanley gets up, passes gas loudly. "Which note was that?" he asks, and goes out into the corridor.

"Funny guy," says Joe.

And the two men continue along the corridor. I have to fight with both my character and my mind, to fly the elevator and write my poems. It doesn't matter that I'm worn out. Old man Darwin smiles, surrounded by Spartan masters. Who are my guardian angels? A few lunatics who wouldn't find peace in paradise. A modest book of poems – that's all I long for. I'm even starting to pray. Is that a sign of strength – or of weakness? I'm losing the energy to look for the answer in books. I'm losing the energy to look for the answer in myself. I am nature's excrescence. Like the Bible says – rip out my eye, cut off my hand. But which eye, which hand? I have a hundred eyes and a hundred hands.

More "back" elevator, more lobby, more number nine. Yes, sir, no, miss, oh yes, the Masons, the Cardinal, the chinchillas. Hop, hop through the meadow, your tail up – isn't that the greatest blessing? With your teeth, your nails, your entire body. And your blood, which is no longer repulsive. And your consciousness, which is no longer there.

Chapter 6

In 1941 Antanas Garšva was a partisan.[41] The Reds were retreating from Kaunas. Their desperate withdrawal, under pressure from the German armies, spawned anarchy. Some of the Reds just threw down their weapons and fell asleep in roadside ditches. They could have been taken prisoner by the gentlest of girls, all they wanted was bread and water. Some of the Reds raped the gentlest of girls and bayoneted those they met. The partisans emerged suddenly. Just like the news of the Reds' retreat.

Skirmishes followed the principle of hide-and-seek. Ruffians leapt from behind trees or bombed bridges, locking with their foes in deadly embraces. Bullets flew from who knows where, sliced through tree leaves and shattered the windows of the summer cottages at Aukštoji Panemunė. And the days crept along – beautiful, clear, still.

Antanas Garšva was on patrol in Artillery Park. He had an assignment: to track whether any Reds were crossing the Nemunas. He lay on the high bank, his rifle by his side, and stared at the water. The sun shone and the sparrows chirped. On the other side of the Nemunas, the sands yellowed, tidily stacked logs browned. Smoke from buildings burning in Kaunas rose up into the clear sky.

Antanas Garšva suddenly heard an unfamiliar sound. A moaning, rhythmic and waning, as though coming from a

41 Following the second Soviet occupation of Lithuania in 1944, the Lithuanian partisans, also known as the Forest Brothers, waged a well-organised guerilla resistance that lasted until 1953. An estimated 30,000 partisans and their supporters were killed.

child or a woman. Ah-oo, ah-oo, ah-oo, ah-oooo. When it broke off, something splashed into the Nemunas. A stray bullet was ending its flight.

Antanas Garšva realised that later. At this moment he glanced back and saw a young Russian, about seventeen years old, with a pleasant face, blue eyes and a messy mop of blonde hair, described in one song as *chubchik kucheryavy*.[42] The young Russian didn't have a gun. His arms were stretched out and he was leaning forward, as though preparing to leap.

Antanas Garšva later spent long hours trying to remember all the details. But he couldn't. The results were engraved in his memory, but he hadn't registered the fierce struggle itself. He could recall only several relief-like details. The smell of sweat; the red fog in his eyes; the sharp rock he had managed to grab; the blows. The stray bullet continued to fly in the syncopated blows. The red fog slunk down from his eyes and wrapped itself around the Red Army soldier's head, and the fog became blood. The smell of sweat became sharper. And Antanas Garšva realised he had a body again. He felt pain on the top of his head, in his stomach, his left arm.

The fog crystallised into a man. There, on the bank of the Nemunas, in the gravel, lay the young Russian's corpse. *Chubchik kucheryavy* had vanished. Antanas Garšva had smashed in a seventeen-year-old's head with a sharp rock. For a while he stared at the dead man's hands. The nails and fingers were losing colour. "I've killed a man," thought Garšva. But these words didn't mean anything. Others, like "the weather is nice today" or "no thank you, I don't drink milk," would have sounded just the same.

*

Temporary peace in the elevator. The Masons are revelling, the Cardinal is dining, the young people's dance will start

---

42 A hairstyle popular with young men at the time, consisting of a thick curly fringe sometimes coming out from under a cap.

at around ten. The occasional guest goes up or down. But you still have to watch the lights: the red square and the green arrow. A poem about geometric shapes? About a stray bullet? The ecstasy of the soul – I was pure soul when I smashed the young Russian's head, and Saint Peter saw the universal church in the four-legged creatures, in the worms and the reptiles, in the birds in the sky... when he was hungry. Drink my blood, eat my body. I am a modern vampire, as helpless as a bat in daylight. A poet who can't write a good poem. Maybe I need to fight? Maybe then my soul would bloom in all the colours of the rainbow?

All I can do is laugh. Out loud. Reality exists. The top of my head, my stomach, my legs, my left arm, they all hurt. For some reason reality likes to beat me over the head, with a fist like a paperweight. And I hit back. The blood of Palaeolithic man still runs in my veins, in my retribution. And I paint my own bison – so that I can kill them. I'm religious. Magic cave paintings and blows with cudgels. Poetic stanzas on paper and a blow with a rock. I was happy after I finished off that young Russian. I dealt with him according to the rules. According to the harmonious laws of battle. My hands glowed with Platonic ideas, with Bergson's *élan vital*. I was Nietzsche's Superman. As that polyglot Hegel would say: the organisation of the world is perfectly rational. The existentialists would probably say that I expressed myself fully, the fatalists that I accurately carried out fate's judgment. The young Russian can choose his own philosophical system. To explain his defeat. Because I am the victor. And I would really like to dance my victory dance, in the desert, by a fire, waving my cudgel. A ritual dance for my God, whom, for an instant, I embodied.

For an instant? But maybe I am coercing myself because I am possessed by a medieval devil? He holds me in an embrace and occasionally squeezes my throat. What's the difference? The hotel, the Nemunas, California, one pole or another. Throats are strangled on all continents. And then an annoying analysis comes in. I, I, I, I – no one else matters. I am the centre of the universe. A frightened god; a god who wishes there were a higher god; a god who would like to become a slave, and, once a slave, be only a god. The psychiatrist will tear off a fresh sheet and write down the name of the illness. Saint Peter will pull out a card inscribed with three words: heaven, purgatory, hell. Which one will he underline? And who could write on my card: be a soul? I should pray? I am praying, I have prayed.

I used to enjoy May services.[43] The incense in the town's wooden church. The roughly cast saints. The melodious bells. The altar boys' red-and-white vestments. The thick wax candles, which I imagined as dead parishioners' *vėlės*.[44]

The flames sputtered a meditation on the eternal. The priest bent at the altar and the cross on his back bent with him. I stared at the starched cloth covering the altar. I listened to the antiphon.

The gaping mouths produced a chanting that was touching in its disharmony. It filtered out the old men's dissonant croaking. A pure hymn floated there, by the cupola. I knelt, my head back. With invisible hands, my God grabbed some angel wings and blew forth the Holy Spirit. He had a double face, like Janus – the left side was Jehovah's, the right Jesus Christ's. That was how I imagined the Holy Trinity.

I inhaled the smell of incense like an ancient Jew. It was Lebanese cedar and the unlocking of the Ark of the Covenant. It was Job, lying face down in the desert. It was the swelling of Red Sea waves. It was the hand of Christ

---

43　Traditional spring services dedicated to the Virgin Mary.

44　In Lithuanian folklore *vėlė* is the term for the spirit of a deceased person, quite distinct from the concept of soul. *Vėlės* were imagined as having some likeness to the deceased and a faint, ethereal physical quality akin to fog. They were thought to live on a high hill and travel on flying benches (*vėlių suoleliai*).

blessing the lepers. His walking on water. His footprints on the road to Golgotha. It was the lamentation of two women. Mary's and Mary Magdalene's. Over the death of their Beloved.

The antiphon. We call to you! To You, to You, to You!

And poor Dostoevsky, who brought together weeping lovers and thought he had found a solution in sexless Alyosha.

The fragments won't come together. They bounce back like the rocks off the adulteress's body in ancient Jerusalem. But they bloody the breasts and the stomach, crush the bones.

Christ does not travel all roads, raising his hand in warning. The fairy tale and human longing do not travel all roads.

Tiny shops carry carefully sorted smaller and larger oranges. Banks contain accounts. Statistical bureaus – the numbers for future weekend accidents. Military headquarters – the annual harvests of new recruits.

My Christ, I bow before You because You longed for a fairy tale. And Plato, I find you a bit ridiculous, with your carefully arranged ideas, like freshly planed boards in a tidy sawmill. You missed the powerful tornados that swept away your tablets. You, of course, are allowed to start everything anew. But first read a bit of your conceptual friend Balzac. Generations pass and are replaced by new ones. And suffering, and madness, and not finding.

And a lonely man standing in the elevator, meditating, clutching the handle. I'm afraid of peace. It envelops me. Fear is better. In hell one can dream about a lost paradise. Yes, it requires enormous vats, satanic faces and boiling tar, cries and the gnashing of teeth, dishevelled hair from old hymn books. And there you have it – a fairy tale about how paradise became paradise, because it was never lost.

The fragments are touching. I can't connect them. Like a child trying to put together cardboard shapes: a road, a stream, hills, a deer. The child clicks his tongue. The landscape comes together.

It's unsettling to stand against a wall and stare at your torturer's hands, empty of stones. This peace is bad. The black candles in the silver candlesticks are bad. This woman, with her unevenly painted cheeks, who neglected to blow the powder off her hooked nose, is bad. The little red carpet under my feet is bad. My foreboding is bad. I don't want peace. I want suffering.

Elena enters the elevator holding a seven-branched candlestick in her hand, the flames trying to jump off it. Elena is a Jerusalem Jew at the Wailing Wall. Elena is a mermaid sewing her detached tail back on. Elena is a kneeling caryatid, with Saint Anne's Church swaying atop her head. Elena is a baseball lost in the grass. Elena is a little girl, how I loved to kiss her.

What did Saint Anthony feel when devils and women didn't haunt him? What did the thousands driven into the gas chambers feel, the runny-nosed Jewish kids screaming at their mother's feet, the mothers chewing their fingers? What did they feel in the Far North, when they froze into stones by felled trees?[45]

> Gnothi seauton[46]
> I thank God, that I was born
> Greek and not barbarian
> Mantike manike
> Noumenon noumenon noumenon
> Epiphenomenon
> Naturalism poetically expressed...
> Associations of mathematicians, chemists
> astronomers, business corporations, labour
> organisations, churches, are trans-
> national because...

---

45 Refers to the harsh living conditions of Lithuanians deported to Siberia during the Soviet occupation.

46 *Gnothi seauton*: Know yourself (Greek).

70

Because I love you *Ilinaa*
Mantike manike
   Nike
No No No Noumenon
Gnothi seauton
Sounds like an avant-garde poem, doesn't it?

Chapter 7

Antanas Garšva just had to turn up North 2nd. He stood at the intersection. There was a drugstore, with an old pharmacist wiping bottles and walking carefully between the aisles. On the other side of the street a sagging old Jewess snoozed amid boxes of fruits and vegetables, snoring lightly as she leaned against the golden oranges.

Garšva waited. He could see the corner of Elena's building. He did not know which apartment was hers. He did not dare cross the street, as that would have made him visible from the windows. The pharmacist glanced sullenly at Garšva a few times, then shuffled towards the register, locked it, put the key in his pocket, and paused by the door to the yard. The drugstore was once robbed, in the middle of the day, by a similar young man with a pleasant face.

Then, unexpectedly, Elena came out. She was wearing a wide, plaid skirt and a white blouse. She looked around, as though unsure of where she was. Garšva strode quickly towards her. The old pharmacist grinned slyly and went back to his bottles. Garšva's steps awakened the Jewess, who let out a wide-mouthed yawn.

They stood before one another.

"Hello," said Garšva.

"Hello."

"Where are you going?"

"To the store."

"There's a park near here. The one where the rabbi was shot. If you have a little time, we could go for a walk. Actually, the rabbi was shot yesterday. It's quiet in the park in the daytime. The rabbi was shot by an eighteen-year-old guy who wanted to hit a moving target. The rabbi was probably meditating with Jehovah. There are benches in the park, and you can see some of the skyscrapers on the other side of the East River. It's eleven now, so say for an hour, an hour and a half?"

Elena looked at Garšva as though he were a stranger.

"I'm having trouble forgetting the trip to Jones Beach," Garšva said. "It was so long ago. The day before yesterday."

"I didn't think you would come," said Elena. The words drifted down, holding their notes.

"Even today, after I woke up, I wasn't sure myself," replied Garšva. "But I wanted to hear about the noblemen's heads."

"Good, then. Let's go. I know your park."

"When those two lie side by side... that was Misha and me," thought the sagging Jewess when the pair passed by her, her eyes glistening with lost dreams.

"This lady has a husband. The husband works, and the lady doesn't work, so she's going to do a bit of work with this fellow," thought the pharmacist. Some time ago his wife left him, and when she died he went to her funeral, he never remarried, he lived alone.

They walked in silence. Elena's bowed head and Garšva's bent shoulders. Dirty Bedford Avenue with its street kiosks filled with Asian immigrant papers, horse-racing types loitering around the soda pop stores, cowboyish youngsters riding bikes festooned with bells and horns, the collapsed sidewalk paving, the smell of onion, garlic, trash, the kind of grey sadness that isn't dispersed by the golden oranges, the golden sun, or the gold watches and rings in the storefronts, or the golden hair of the girl standing in the dry cleaner's doorway, or the blue strip of sky peeking through gaps down the side streets.

And the two came to the large square that Garšva had called a park. There were baseball diamonds, cement walls for hitting balls, sparse trees, grass, benches. They sat down. And they saw, in front of them, gasoline cisterns, a school building, a few skyscraper towers.

"This will be our only meeting. You are mistaken about me. My husband and I are a model couple."

"Forgive me. I'll go, if you want."

Garšva's hand grasped the arm of the park bench.

"I'll be on my way."

"Why?"

Surprised, Garšva stared at Elena's eyes. True peace, and a calm curiosity, and a bit of the maternal.

"Why?" repeated Elena. "This is the only time we will meet alone. My husband invited you to visit, and so do I."

"I didn't want to insult you," said Garšva.

"I know," replied Elena.

Garšva got out his cigarettes and they both lit up.

"I'll be honest. I'm looking for something."

"I've heard about you."

"Really? What exactly?"

"I've heard that you're a womaniser."

"That's the least of it. They say I'm destructive, that I wallow in my own misery. I repeat: I'm searching for something. For a week now I've been searching for a few stanzas."

"I like your poems. They're true in their incompleteness."

"I don't know how to end things. I need peace. My world is falling apart. I'm detail-oriented. I don't like to buy things in bulk, but I cherish fragments. I want to describe sliding into the abyss. Right now I'm looking for a solution. There's this boy in my new poem. His mother is dying in the next room. The door is locked, the boy isn't allowed in. He's watching a blue fly crawl along the wall. Soon the fly will reach the window, which is slightly open. Will it fly out, or stay in the room?"

"If I understand you to some degree, then ... it will fly out. And when the little boy is let in to see his dying mother, he'll be sad about the blue fly, because it flew off."

Elena's words had a new, brittle tone.

"Thank you for the gift," said Garšva. Elena glanced at him quizzically, and there was fear in her eyes.

"I wasn't mistaken. I knew I needed your help. That time, in the car, you decided that the nun and I got lost because of the dead noblemen's heads. I understood intuitively: you will solve the problem of the boy in the closed room."

"I'm just a former high school teacher. And I love Vilnius," said Elena. She carefully extinguished her cigarette with the heel of her shoe, and Garšva noticed that her right stocking was on crookedly again today. He noticed that her face powder had been applied unevenly, that her eyebrows had been extended too thickly, her lips painted more brightly, so that Elena was no longer the little grey woman she had been the day before yesterday at Jones Beach. A moment ago there had been fear in her greyish eyes, and Garšva knew this look. From the mirror he used to look at when the invisible hands started choking him.

"I know. Memories mean old age. Oh no, I am thirty-two years old. I meant old age figuratively. And I'm angry. Some ladies I know talk a lot about the past. They remember fashions, faces, dish sets, maids. But I remember the noblemen's heads, the statues on the roof of the Cathedral, the stone wall by Rasų Cemetery, the columns of the Vilnius University courtyard... I am just like my acquaintances."[47]

She fell silent, she contemplated the skyscraper towers. Garšva shifted, and she said, "I can guess what you're going to suggest. I read your poems and articles. I tried to retrace your steps. Yes, I saw Modigliani's reclining woman in a tiny gallery. The magical yellowishness, the Byzantine sadness, as you wrote. You quoted Cocteau, a fresco related to the ones in the temples at Luxor. At the Museum of Modern Art I looked at your Soutine, the congealed blood in the folds of a young Jewish boy's clothing. At the Metropolitan I tried to see the ornamental purity of the Persian miniatures. And in the Museum of Natural History I found a copy of a round head, an ancient meteor that had fallen in the desert, just as you wrote. I won't go to look at them any more."

47   Elena is referring to well-known Vilnius landmarks.

"Why not?"

"I won't go to look at them any more," Elena repeated.

Garšva shifted.

"You want to run off again?" asked Elena, and Garšva stuffed his hands into his pockets.

"Not at all. I just feel a little excited. You are a reader who remembers entire sentences. And you say that you won't go back to look at them any more."

Elena laughed. For the first time Garšva had a good look at her teeth. Fine, even, bluish. With good quality fillings. He once again heard a brittle tone in her laugh.

"How old are you?"

"Forty-one."

"How childish you are! I imagined an ironic character. And you get excited like a high school student."

"Put your hands on your purse," said Garšva coldly. "If I'm excited and stuffed my hands into my pockets, so that I wouldn't clutch the bench, then you should not crumple your skirt. You would do better to crumple the leather of your purse."

A faint blush broke through the layer of powder, fingers trembled and froze clutching skirt folds. Sharp shoe heels bore into the gravel. Leg muscles, and the ones around the lips, tightened. This went on for a few seconds and then Elena's body gradually relaxed, and she leaned back like a worker on a break.

"Forgive me. I'm a poet, but I can also be terribly prosaic," Garšva said softly.

Elena did not reply. Two fat pigeons were strolling along the path, lazily swaying their stomachs like pregnant women. A black-haired boy flew by like a madman on a red bicycle. A silver sweetie wrapper sparkled annoyingly on the ground.

"Tell me about your Vilnius," said Garšva. Elena's eyelashes were wet. She was still leaning back against the bench, the remnants of a meagre smile playing on her closed lips.

"You're mistaken. I wasn't disappointed by your poems and articles. That's my own fault. They make me feel my past more strongly. When I looked at your artists and took in your images, I saw my own Vilnius more clearly, and it was painful. I had thought that my memories would comfort me until my death. Your writing forces one to suffer. It's like pouring boiling oil on a wound."

"You are my second reader."

"Who is the first?"

"I myself."

Elena stood up, and the fat pigeons weren't startled. They turned their little heads, and their tiny beadlike eyes went brown.

"I'm going home," said Elena.

"You haven't told me about them," said Garšva, still seated. Elena was smoothing out the folds of her plaid skirt.

"I'm going home. I have to pick up a few things, prepare dinner."

"You haven't told me about them," said Garšva, now standing. One of the pigeons staggered off, the other continued to look around with its little bead eyes.

"You stay here. I'll go back alone."

Elena bent her head. A fold in her neck revealed a brown mole that looked like a pigeon's eye.

"Forgive me. I can't stay any longer. Maybe, some day, some other time."

Garšva noticed that Elena's eyelashes were even wetter. He took her hand and she didn't pull it back.

"Tomorrow?" whispered Garšva.

The pigeons flew off.

The deaf bouncing of a ball against the cement wall echoed from the playgrounds, the sun turned, the little silver wrapper no longer sparkled, the narrow ladder on the cistern shone, and Elena asked, "Is it necessary?"

Garšva looked at her now dryer eyes and his answer corresponded with the echo of a ball. "Yes, it's necessary."

"At what time?"

"I start work tomorrow at four thirty in the afternoon. If ten o'clock works for you…"

"I'll be here at ten," said Elena, and Garšva let go of her hand.

"Don't walk with me. I want to go back alone. Goodbye."

"Goodbye."

"I knew you would come," Elena said unexpectedly. And walked off. With small, hurried steps. The plaid skirt rustled as it moved away. And Garšva watched the grey hair and the white blouse. Until Elena turned on to Bedford Avenue.

*

Antanas Garšva lets off a small group of aged boxers. They're riding from floor to floor, glasses of whisky in their hands, visiting each other's identical rooms. They laugh too hard, and with clenched fists imitate the blows they gave and received years ago. On his way out, a stocky man with the narrowest forehead and flattened ears gives Garšva a little punch in the shoulder. Garšva sways with his whole body and touches the stocky man's chest with his fist. The little group laughs. "Go for it, boy! Give it to him. He was kissing the ground in the second round." And one of them presses a quarter into Garšva's hand. They go off down the corridor, swaying side to side, still feeling young and strong from the whisky. Garšva closes the elevator door.

Chapter 8

During the first Bolshevik occupation, Antanas Garšva wasn't able to publish his poems or articles in any of the Soviet newspapers or magazines.[48] His work was called reactionary and formalist. Garšva and his father lived in the summer cottage at Aukštoji Panemunė. It was a small cottage. Four rooms, a kitchen, a glassed-in porch. A surveyor and his wife rented two of the rooms; quiet people who played chess in their spare time.

Garšva's father would mope around the garden, lingering by the pear trees (the ones he had once ordered from Denmark), fingering the green fruit. The Bolsheviks had cut off his pension because he was a Knight of the Order of Gediminas, an honour that, as a distinguished Lithuanian government official, he had once been forced to purchase. Garšva's father spoke little to Garšva. The fingering of the pears was a reduced version of that earlier meditation on the bank of the Nemunas, when his father had gazed at Pažaislis Monastery. Now Russian soldiers meditated there, bayonets thrust on to the ends of their rifles, shouting "Away!" to anyone who approached. His father didn't touch his violin any more. It hung on the wall gathering dust, and the one time his father strummed a chord it must have echoed loudly in his heart because he grimaced as though he had tasted something bitter, and he strode out to the garden, his hand on his chest – an old-fashioned courtier bearing a declaration of love.

That calm summer evening Garšva was sitting in the glassed-in porch, writing. Acacia bushes grew just outside, a wooden fence separated the little world of the cottage

48   See note 5.

from the quiet street. A lamp with a bell-shaped shade stood on a cross-legged table. A nightingale trilled in the evening calm.

Certain poets have mercilessly embellished this vigorous, syncopated decline, Garšva thought to himself. He remembered the old Lithuanian polyphonies his father had once hummed, so true in their lyric atonality. Then serfdom was imposed, and later, all the freed slaves could do was try to compete with their masters: by harmonising their songs and importing a brittle Olympus to the North.[49] Perkūnas, Pykuolis, Patrimpas, high priests and priestesses, imported southern gods and their servants quickly donned Lithuanian folk costumes.[50]

Lole palo eglelo
Lepo leputeli
Lo eglelo
Lepo leputeli
....
Skambinoj kankleliai
Lioj ridij augo.[51]

The nightingale's ancient song. Jehovah had neglected this land, had focused all of his attention on Asia Minor.

---

49 Serfdom was introduced in Lithuania in 1447 by Kazimieras Jogailaitis, Grand Duke of Lithuania and King of Poland. The oppression of the serfs became heavier in 1795, when Lithuania was annexed by Imperial Russia. Reforms abolishing serfdom were introduced in 1861 and intensified following the Uprising of 1863.

50 Perkūnas, Pykuolis, Patrimpas: the ancient Baltic gods of air/ lightning, the dead, and nature/fertility.

51 These refrains appear at various points in the novel. They evoke archaic Lithuanian polyphonic song, and have no literal meaning, except for the phrases, *skambinoj kankleliai* (the zithers rang) and *augo* (it grew).

...

The room had white plaster walls. An unpainted table stood by the window. Two chairs. A cheap felt hat with a soaked brim hung on a nail. Antanas Garšva noticed a heavy paperweight, with fake marble veins, on the table, next to a stained inkpot.

...

Triangular firs, Lithuanian temple spires, rose to the stars from impenetrable bogs. Gliding mists; dishevelled fairies; small, shabby *kaukai*; sprites whirring through the air; field and farm deities wrung from the earth. Abstract nature gods, perpetually changing shape.

Lole palo eglelo
Lepo leputėli, –

trilled the nightingale. One had only to stand deep in the forest and watch the grass snakes hugging the ground, the toads contemplating the universe through their bulging eyes. One had only to meditate, suspending thought. Words were still magical formulae. As mysterious and meaningful as the formation of the mists. One had only to watch the sharp-tongued flames of the eternal fire: they lit up the firs – the towers – in the shrine of the great, immeasurable earth. To be born, to live, to die. To dissolve in the mists, to climb up on to high benches, to sometimes wander through familiar forests and marshes.[52]

And if sadness and fear should descend, one could whittle pieces of wood into half-human carvings and place them by the roadsides.[53] Sad fear sculpted into the long wrinkles, the shortened torsos, a final surrender to the earth. These wooden sculptures did not compete with nature. Personifications recognisable in the embraces of

52 See note 64 re. *vėlės*.
53 Reference to traditional Lithuanian wooden sculptures (*dievukai*) depicting a pensive Christ (*Rūpintojėlis* – "the Sorrowful One") or other saints, often placed at roadsides.

gnarled trunks, tangled roots, the movements of lakes and rivers. A sad fear protecting the living.

Skambinoj kankleliai
Lioj ridij augo, –
trilled the nightingale.

Honeycombs, rye ears, rue, tulips and lilies. Lazy, sweet-toothed bears. Pine resin – golden amber, Baltic foam slowly dissolving into the amber sand.

...

With the back of his hand, Garšva once more wiped the blood that continued to flow from his nose. He glanced at his hand, then at the inkpot. The inkpot was full of black ink. Simutis sighed deeply.

"You tossed it into the Nemunas? Zuika was right. It's a good thing you're an idiot. Only an idiot would go to the bus station that same morning."

"I had two weeks," Garšva replied, sniffling.

"In the veranda," said Simutis.

...

The wicket gate swung open. Two men entered the veranda and stood before Garšva. Two greenish silhouettes outlined by the light of the table lamp. The world of the past sunk into non-existence. Antanas Garšva stood up, pressing his hands against the table.

"Hello, Comrade Garšva," said the poet Zuika. During the years of independence he had written occasional poems. About war, about Vilnius, about national holidays. The poems contained plenty of exclamation marks and frequently repeated the word "Lithuania". And he was still writing commissioned poems. About war, about Moscow, about Communist holidays. These poems were not that different. They contained plenty of exclamation marks and frequently repeated the word "Stalin".

Zuika was a short man with a handsome face, a small head, hair of an ambiguous colour, and eyes red from insomnia or drink. He had plump, feminine hands, clean and manicured. He looked at them continuously. Garšva didn't recognise the second man. Tall and broad-shouldered, with prominent cheekbones, a low forehead and a strong chin, he looked more like a factory foreman.

"Comrade Simutis. He spent four years in prison," stated Zuika. A plump hand flew out and back, as though Zuika were a policeman directing traffic.

"Sit down," said Garšva, seating himself. Zuika positioned himself on the bench, Simutis leaned against the veranda window frame and placed his right foot on the rustic white bench. His foot, in its hard, black shoe, was disproportionately long.

"Don't be surprised that we have dropped in on you at night," said Zuika in his smooth tenor voice. Garšva was confused. He barely knew Zuika, so the man's familiar tone surprised him. Zuika snatched up the sheet of handwriting. Suddenly they were children. Garšva lunged for the sheet, but Zuika hid it behind his back. Simutis quickly sat down on the bench between Garšva and Zuika. The sheet reappeared and Zuika read it out loud, his lips quivering with sarcasm.

"A typical blend of decadence and bourgeois folklore," said Zuika.

"It's the first draft. Just the beginning of a poem," replied Garšva, instantly realising that, for some reason, he was justifying himself. Then he spoke calmly, as though scanning his words.

"What right do you have to come here at night and check on me?"

"Calm down. The working people have the right to inspect. And Comrade Simutis here works for the glorious NKVD."

The plump little hand repeated the policeman's gesture. For a moment they were all silent. "I am not obliged to be afraid," thought Garšva, and then spoke:

"If I remember correctly, a stanza in one of your poems went like this:

Now freedom's bell rings high
We know how to preserve it!
And the rifleman's[54] name we cry
Like a brother's or a friend's.
Then a week ago I read another version:
Now freedom's bell rings high
We know how to preserve it!
And Stalin's name we sigh
Like a father's or a friend's.
Your technique is improving. The rhyme 'sigh' is more perfect that 'cry.' Congratulations."

Simutis looked at Zuika askance.

"Did you know that the head of the Riflemen's League threatened me?" squealed Zuika. "And not just me – my elderly parents too! He said he would drive them out of their little farm and make beggars of them. So I had to give in, but you should know: the first version was the second one, and I changed the words. I was forced to. I'd been writing about Stalin for several years, while you were still chasing decaying isms!"

"How many times did I see you in a restaurant with the head of the Riflemen's League? I suppose he paid your tab by force?!" asked Garšva, grinning.

"Lies!" was all Zuika could manage.

Simutis took the manuscript sheet and began to read.

"I don't quite understand it," he said in a weary baritone.

"And you won't understand. It's all verbal acrobatics, encoded with bourgeois propaganda," said Zuika, cutting in.

Simutis stared at the sheet as though it were illegible.

"I'm pulling myself together. I have to find a way out of this," thought Garšva, and said, "The matter is simple, Comrade Simutis. What you see here is something in an embryonic state. I want to write a poem on the topic of folk song. But unfortunately, my technique is weak – I can't

---

54   Reference to the Lithuanian Riflemen's League, a volunteer
     civic defense organisation founded in 1919.

compare myself with dear Zuika – so I need multiple drafts. When I'm done, the poem will be accessible to the people."

"He's trying to get away with it. He's sitting on two chairs," said Zuika, glancing towards Simutis. His plump hands rested on the table, their soft dimples and carefully filed nails more distinct under the table lamp.

"It appears that dear Zuika takes very good care of his nails – something that is not typical of a proletarian poet," said Garšva softly. Zuika twisted his delicate fingers. Simutis put the sheet on the table and spoke.

"I don't understand everything, but I like it. When I was a child, in the countryside, I heard folk singing. It was nice. It was nice to listen to them in the evening. This is also a song. A folk song, I'm thinking. If you show the people suffering under their masters, and the people are singing... And if at the end Stalin's sun shines bright, then I think it will do. All the great poets wrote about the people. Strazdelis, Donelaitis?"[55]

"That is correct, Comrade Simutis."

"Very well. Give it a go. But don't forget. There is no more oppression. The future is bright. I'd like to read this poem when you're done with it. How long will it take you?"

"I suppose a week, maybe two."

"Good. Then let's say that in two weeks you bring me your poem, Comrade Garšva," decided Simutis. He got up, as did Garšva. Zuika stayed seated, his little fingers now still.

"I hope you'll be one of us," said Simutis warmly, pressing Garšva's hand.

"Comrade Simutis, I'll explain..." sputtered Zuika, getting up.

"We'll sort everything out in two weeks. Let's go. Goodnight, Comrade Garšva."

"Goodnight."

...

---

55 Lithuanian poets, Antanas Strazdas (1760–1833) and Kristijonas Donelaitis (1714–1780).

The single window was covered with a grate. On either side of it hung once-bright cotton curtains. An enamel spittoon stood in the corner. Yellow cigarette butts floated in a yellow mucous porridge. Cigarette butts also lay on the long-unpolished parquet. Simutis caught Garšva's eye.

"Now you're going to kneel down at the spittoon and lick up those butts with your tongue," he said, and sat down on the edge of the table. Garšva sniffled. The blood was still flowing. He heard a car horn and noticed a blue fly. It was crawling, slowly, up the window grate.

"Faster!"

The nightingale trilled. She wasn't the secretary of a proud or overly emotional poet. She was just a nightingale. *Lole palo eglelo* – a polyphony. The gliding mists – spirits of the dead. A fairy tale – a forgotten language.

Antanas Garšva wrote. A calm inevitability flowed back into his unconscious. The nightingale fell silent. Above the fence it brightened. In the nightingale's song, in himself, Garšva was searching for a lost world. Just as this modest bird had sung a thousand years ago. Its song a cipher, the first communicated code.

Garšva whistled, imitating the sleeping bird. "I'm writing a fairy tale. I believe in Ariadne's thread, I believe in intuition. I'll leave resurrecting the past to scholars of ancient religions. They can argue amongst themselves." Two stanzas of a poem lived on a piece of cheap paper. Trees and shrubs grew in a lost world. Fir, pine, linden, oak, birch, juniper.

...

Simutis slipped off the table and stood facing Garšva.

"I'm waiting."

Garšva was silent. He took a blow to the hollow of his stomach and collapsed to the ground. Consciousness faded and returned. He noticed a stench. He had lost control of his bowels.

"Did it in your pants, Mister Poet?"

...

The two men left. The little gate swung shut. A reddish glow gushed over Artillery Park. Garšva crumpled the page of manuscript and stuffed it into his pocket. "I've got to run, get away. To the country." He turned off the lamp. Went back into the house. Opened the door of his father's bedroom. His father's nightshirt was unbuttoned, a tuft of grey chest hair rising rhythmically. His father slept with his mouth open. It reeked of old man's sweat. A red blanket shifted at his feet. Let him sleep. I'll take off without saying goodbye. Garšva closed the door. He put on an old jacket and went into the kitchen. He drank two glasses of milk. Ate a slice of bread. Then he lit a cigarette and went out into the street. He walked along the Nemunas, ripping up the crumpled sheet. He threw the shreds of paper into the water. The shreds floated, whirling, towards the bridge.

...

Garšva tried to get up. He could barely breathe. He could not move his torso or legs. Then he began to walk on his hands, dragging his lower body. Like a dog whose back legs had been hit by a car. Towards the spittoon. He even growled, like a dog. Just two more metres to the spittoon. Garšva paused.

"Faster!"

"Long live Babochkin," Garšva muttered.[56]

"Who's that?"

"He did a good job playing Chapaev."

Simutis grabbed the heavy paperweight from the table.

"Are you going to crawl?"

"Don't hit me! Don't hit me!" shrieked Garšva. He crawled another few inches. The spittoon was right there. His arms began to shake, and he collapsed to the floor.

"Get up," said Simutis.

---

56 Boris Babochkin (1904–1975), a Russian film actor and director. Best known for playing the lead character in the 1934 film *Chapaev*, about a Red Army commander during the Russian Civil War.

"Long live Babochkin," Garšva whispered.

Quivering, he raised himself. All he could feel was fear. I'll do anything, anything, even stick my tongue in it, for him not to hit me!

Simutis's shoe was right by his nose. The smell of shoe polish was sharper than that of Garšva's faeces. Garšva looked up, smiled childishly and, staring at Simutis's noble chin, said, "Don't want to."

Simutis smashed the paperweight on to the top of his head.

...

Antanas Garšva came to in the veranda. He was lying on the bench, Simutis and a man in a white coat stood before him.

"Are you awake?" asked Simutis.

Garšva blinked.

"Good. I spared you. Do you hear what I'm saying?"

"I hear. You spared me."

"Good. Now listen. You were walking along May 1st Street. You wanted to cross to the other side. You can't remember anything else. Repeat what I said."

"I was walking along May 1st Street. Wanted to cross to the other side. Can't remember anything else."

"Correct. You were hit by a bus. Understood?"

"Understood. I was hit by a bus."

"Good. When you recover, you'll continue to write."

"Good. I'll write."

"I like you. I got carried away. But... I think it'll do you good. I think you'll be one of us. Get better. Write."

Simutis and the man in the white coat left. Beyond the fence a car started. Garšva touched his head. It was bandaged.

...

Antanas Garšva recovered. He was left with a winding scar on his crown. He began to write a long article, "Humanism in Soviet Literature", but never completed it. The Germans invaded Lithuania. For about two years Garšva worked at a publishing house. He did copy-editing and no longer wrote.

First his father died. He would pick his nose for hours, not saying a word, then, later, began moaning. He was taken to hospital. His father died of bladder cancer, but only after a lengthy struggle, because he had a strong heart. The surveyor and his wife moved out. Antanas Garšva ended up alone.

Peace gradually enveloped him. He forgot which day or hour it was. He would fall asleep at the table. He ignored his fellow writers' queries. And then, one day, he stopped going to the publishing house.

His colleagues brought a doctor to see him. The doctor decided: Garšva is not dangerous, he doesn't need to be taken to the hospital. The doctor occasionally visited from the city, as did some of the writers, carrying meagre parcels of food, or money that couldn't buy anything. Garšva began to speak again. In a brief, condensed way. The doctor and the writers decided: Garšva will recover.

It was early autumn, and he would wander around the garden. Often he would pick a leaf from a cherry tree and stare at it for a long time. It was a map. He was searching for lost territories in the leaf of a cherry tree.

The veins in a cherry leaf – a stone wall as solid as a Roman senator's nose. Surrounded by grass. Caesar knelt, writing on a tablet. *Gallia omnis est divisa in partes tres.*[57] The barbarians placed wreaths on their heads. Green ones. It was a celebration. Where? By the sea. *Lole? Lepo. Eglelo? Lalo.* You are right, ancient Aestus.[58] Spend hours staring at your Baltic Sea. At a leaf from a cherry tree. And with as little emotion as possible. "Wrapped broadly in the western

---

57 All Gaul is divided into three parts (Latin).

58 Aestus: the Aesti were an ancient Baltic people, first referred to in this way by the Roman historian Tacitus in his treasise *Germania*, ca. 98 CE.

waves" – not for me.[59] Short, crooked pines by the sea. Sap slithers down the trunk, the sand, and the waves carry off the sap. A precious stone in Venetian lace. A Roman senator holds a piece of amber in his palm. "It is more beautiful than gold," says the senator, because the chests are filled with sesterce, and there is only one piece of amber. *Augo? Ridij. Skambino? Palo.* Ancient Aestus, musical Aestus, show me your own tree, the one you prayed to. Does it command? No. Does it comfort? Yes. Look at the smoke rising to the sky, at the wisp of grass, at the soaring bird. At the cherry leaf. You can.

Garšva often had diarrhoea. He would run to the wooden outhouse – his father had carved a lopsided heart in the door. Garšva would sit there, staring at a heart-shaped patch of sky.

"Flood my breast with your chilly wave," he would recite.[60] And would think to himself that he should finish the poem he had shredded and tossed into the Nemunas. But he didn't have the strength. They were only words. *Lalo*, ancient Aestus, the Roman nose, *skambinoj*, sky, amber. Within a month the doctor had cured his diarrhoea.

* * *

Ženia arrived one evening, tidy, not much aged, as is often the case with petite women.[61] Garšva was sitting in the veranda. A small pile of acacia branches lay on the bench. He was holding one of the branches, picking off the leaves and tossing them, like someone playing "loves me, loves me not".

"Hi there, handsome," said Ženia. "I heard you were sick. One of your friends mentioned it."

---

59 *"Išsisupus plačiai vakarų vilnimis,"* from the poem "Nuo Birutės kalno" ("From Birutė's Hill", 1895) by the Lithuanian poet Maironis (1862–1932).

60 *"Mano krutinę užliek savo šalta banga,"* from Maironis's poem.

61 Ženia is the Lithuanian spelling of Zhenia, the diminutive of the popular Russian name Evgenija.

Garšva grinned, and continued to pick the leaves in silence. Ženia put her bag on the table.

"I've brought some butter, bacon and eggs. I haven't forgotten you, handsome."

"That's great," said Garšva.

"Nice place. Can I take a look inside?"

"Go ahead," Garšva offered.

A few minutes later, Ženia returned.

"Not bad. It needs a cleaning."

"Go ahead," Garšva agreed, pruning the last branch. Ženia gently stroked Garšva's neck.

"Can I move in with you? You're alone, right?"

"Yes, alone. But I don't have much to eat."

"Don't you worry. We'll make ourselves some food."

"We'll make ourselves some."

"I think this place will do," she said, as though to herself.

"Oh yes, it'll do," agreed Garšva.

"Do you know what?" asked Ženia, surprised.

"What?"

"What I'm thinking?"

"I'm guessing it's something nice?"

Ženia looked at Garšva carefully.

"Say – one."

"One."

"Two."

"Two."

"How much is two times two?"

"Four?"

"And twelve plus fifteen?"

"Twenty-seven? Are you studying arithmetic?"

"It looks like you're ok," Ženia concluded. Then suddenly leaned towards him and whispered, "Say: I am Antanas Garšva."

"I am Antanas Garšva. Always was and always will be. Forever and ever, Amen," whispered Garšva.

"You're almost fine. I'll make some eggs."

That night Garšva remembered things he had forgotten. He slept with Ženia, and devoured four eggs and bacon for breakfast.

On the second day of her stay, Ženia revealed why she was there. It was evening and a full, yellow moon hung over Artillery Park. The acacias infused the warm fall air. The dried-out veranda bench creaked. A few slices of bread and some butter lay on the table. Ženia got up and began to clear the table. When she had placed everything on a wooden tray, she spoke, "Turn on the light." Garšva pressed the button. Ženia wiped the tabletop.

"I'm opening my business tomorrow," she announced.

"You're setting up a shop? Don't bother. There aren't any goods these days, and shoppers won't visit such a remote place."

Ženia's eyes flashed angrily.

"Are you really crazy, or do you just act like you are?"

"Sometimes I think I've always been this way."

Garšva turned away from her. He stared at the full moon through the glass panes of the veranda.

"Listen, handsome. I'm still in the same business."

"Oh," said Garšva, staring at the full moon. It sat on the chimney of the barracks lock-up, looking like a stick person drawn by a child.

"Listen – I want to do some business here. We'll both make some money."

"You'll pay rent?"

"You'll be well fed, I'll keep you clothed, and you won't have to pay me."

"A heavenly proposition."

"So you agree?"

"And what kind of clientele are you aiming for?"

"Germans. Don't worry, I don't service regular soldiers. My brand is rising."

Garšva laughed.

"My friend the baker is director of a tobacco factory.

Members of the corps de ballet are distributing apartments and issuing orders for materials. A clarinettist from Bremen is conducting Handel. A musician from the town of Bremen. He told me about how one farmer traded flour for a piano and now spends the entire day banging out a dance tune with one finger. Russian prisoners of war are clearing his fields. I recently read about this kind of scene in a weekly paper. The description contained multiple uses of the words 'someone' and 'for some reason'. What rank of officer do you service?"

"You're seriously crazy," said Ženia, sadly.

"Get out," said Garšva calmly.

"You ate my bacon and eggs, and now you tell me to get out!" growled Ženia.

"There's a gold-plated cigarette case in my room. Take it and get out," Garšva said even more quietly.

The full moon floated away from the chimney. A heavenly Picasso had shattered the naive harmony. Cool air was forcing its way in through the open window. Garšva closed it shut. He wanted to say "Get out" one more time, but the calm that had wrapped itself around him was stronger. Garšva smiled, like the childish moon hanging over Artillery Park.

"I'm going to write a good poem," he said gently.

"I'm starting to understand transcendence. The mist. The mist off the town marsh. The misty polyphonies. The mist in my head. Real mist. Mist gives birth to the word, it's a phonetic mist… and what do you think, Ženia? I'll use the marshes, I'll use the pensive Christ, I'll use *lo eglelo*, I'll use – what else should I use? Eh, Ženia?"[62]

"Crazy idiot," whispered Ženia.

"What else should I use, what else should I grab? Eh, Ženia?"

---

62 Pensive Christ: refers to a *Rūpintojėlis* (Sorrowful One), a traditional Lithuanian wooden statue of a pensive Christ figure.

"Why don't you grab your… ," she snapped and went inside. Garšva went out. He forgot about the full moon, which had glided over his house. The chimney of the barracks lock-up rose up straight, like a regular chimney. Garšva broke off an acacia branch.

Ženia stayed. She installed a wood stove in the veranda and hung army blankets on the windows. Two more girls moved into Garšva's house: fair-haired, cheerful, buxom. It was a model bordello. Drunken songs echoed. The Germans were happy to drive to the countryside. Garšva's literary colleagues ended up on the gravel road when they tried to liberate him. Ženia would bring her clients into the veranda and explain, in her broken German:

"He is a famous Lithuanian poet. The Bolsheviks tortured him horribly. They hit him on the head with a hammer, slowly, until he turned into an idiot. But he isn't dangerous. He even writes. He is grateful to the German army … for the liberation."[63]

The clients would scrutinise the smiling Garšva and offer him cognac. Garšva would drink, say "*Ich danke Ihnen recht schoen*" and shake their hands.[64] Then he would explain that Ženia and the German army had rescued him from squalor and that he was perfectly happy because he was free to meditate on transcendence. He would write an important book. It would contain a cycle of poems celebrating the glorious German army and its

---

63 Following the first Soviet occupation of Lithuania (1940), many Lithuanians, still reeling from the mass deportations begun by the Soviets, hoped that the advance of the German army would lead to the restoration of Lithuania's independence, or at least autonomy. These hopes were soon quashed when Nazi authorities established full administrative control of the country, using lower-level Lithuanian bureaucrats for rubber-stamping purposes. The German occupation lasted until the second Soviet occupation in Summer 1944.

64 *Ich danke Ihnen recht schoen*: Thank you very much (German).

brilliant leader. He was a follower of the greatest mystic –
Friedrich Nietzsche.

The customers agreed that Garšva was an intelligent
madman and paid Ženia a higher fee, or brought impressive
packages of food. "We are not Ivans – we are cultured
people," they would say.

The bordello was shut down unexpectedly. One of the
girls stole a sergeant major's gold watch. Ženia and the girls
were thrown into prison, and Garšva's colleagues had him
admitted to hospital.

...

Garšva remembered distinctly the clear winter morning on
which he fully regained consciousness. He woke up and
glanced at the floor. It was scattered with green leaves.
Garšva looked out the window. Thick snow blanketed
the roofs. And beyond, white-capped Kaunas Cathedral.
Garšva understood that he was in a hospital room. It was
long, narrow, brown-walled. A metal bed, a little table, and
a window – covered in a grate. Garšva threw off the blanket
and sat up in the bed. He stroked his striped pyjamas. Then
he picked up a leaf from the floor. It was made of paper. On
the table lay thin wires with bits of green paper wound into
them. Imitating tree branches. Garšva found the bell and
pressed it. A nurse entered the room, a tall, older woman
with the face of a nun.

"Good morning," said Garšva.

"Good morning, Mr Garšva."

Garšva was still holding a paper leaf.

The nurse was observing him searchingly.

"What does this mean?"

"It's your favourite occupation."

"I've been picking leaves from these wires?"

"A lot of the time. Occasionally, you wrote."

"Can I take a look?"

The nurse opened the drawer of the little table and
pulled out several pages of close handwriting. Garšva took

them. He read, and the nurse stood watching him. He read
out loud:
"Lole palo bitch gravel
Sio Se Senator's fate
No? A leaf has a colour
No? You are mistaken, madam."
"Was I like this… for a long time?"
"Quite a while. Several months."
"Could I speak to the doctor?"
"Right away."
The nurse left. Garšva got up. A pocket mirror flashed
in the open drawer. Garšva looked at himself. His hair had
been shorn. A long winding scar ran down from the top
of his head. Garšva saw a grey face, a few days' stubble,
unfamiliar lines around his mouth, a sagging chin. A doctor
entered the room. A round, angelic face, slicked back hair,
attractive in his clean coat.
"How are you feeling, my dear colleague?"
"I'm… not a doctor," said Garšva, and placed the papers
and mirror in the drawer.
"But I… am a poet. You have inspired me. You've been
reciting folk songs. I return to the manor and meet an old
woman carrying two bright candles," recited the doctor,
like a high-spirited police chief acting in the play *The
Murderer's Son*.
"How do you feel?" he asked, now more seriously.
Garšva swept his hand across his pyjamas.
"There's a veranda, yes, the veranda of a summer cottage,
a full moon, this girl, a German soldier with a bottle and…
I think I'm saying something about Nietzsche."
Garšva laughed suddenly. Then continued, apologetically.
"Oh, forgive me, doctor. A delayed reaction. You
addressed me as your colleague. I understand, I had lost my
senses. And how are you feeling?"
"I like you today," the doctor exclaimed cheerfully. "But
call me Doctor Ignas. That's what everyone here calls me."

A month later Garšva was released. And when the Bolsheviks returned to Lithuania, he fled to Germany.

*

The elevator goes up, the elevator goes down. Not all of his memories return. A partial amnesia remains. The polyphonies and the nightingale have travelled to the depths of his unconscious. The spring snow has melted. No more footprints in the steaming earth. But a new craving to retrieve the damp fragrance of the acacias, the nightingale, the ancient signs. I am like a scientist who has lost his formulae. And I don't want to write a popular pamphlet. I must start again. Wait for a winter consciousness, for snow.

I want to go back to that evening in Aukštoji Panemunė, to the veranda. I need geometric mercy. Mysticism. Judgment.

We gather in the Valley of Josaphat. I arrive in a blue bus. It's good that it's blue. That's a sign of hope. The driver won't answer my questions, but I don't mind, it's best not to speak to bus drivers. I'm not being shown the passing sights. The windows of the bus are opaque. And the driver is blocked off by black fabric. Finally, we stop. I get off. The bus drives away.

The Valley of Josaphat is paved in cement and enclosed by a stone wall. It is the size of a room. A gate opens in the wall and three judges enter the valley. They are wearing judges' robes, their parchment faces set off by white wing collars. The middle one opens a thick book and begins.

"Your name?"

"Antanas Garšva."

"Profession?"

"Poet and unsuccessful earthling."

"Your worldview?"

"Unarticulated."

"What was the worldview you were born into?"

"Formally, the believers' one, but…"

"No comments, please," interrupts the judge.

"Did you follow the commandments?"

"It's possible that I didn't follow them in strict terms, but…"

"Comments are unnecessary," the judge interrupts again. "Did you follow the commandments as you were taught them?"

"It appears not."

"Very well. According to paragraph eight you are slated for liquidation. Thank you for your replies."

"Could you please tell me what it says in paragraph eight?"

"It's a rather long paragraph. In short: anyone who failed to follow the commandments is liquidated. For example. The faithful – those for the faithful, atheists – those for atheists, liars – those for liars, murderers – those for murderers, cowards – those for cowards, moralisers – those for moralisers. And those who followed the commandments are transferred to Heaven."

"I followed the commandments for seekers."

Now the three judges laugh rhythmically. Like members of an opera chorus.

"There is no such category in the Valley of Josaphat."

"Forgive me. One more question. Why was I brought here in a blue bus? That colour inspires hope."

But the judges can't answer in time. Antanas Garšva is already at the bottom, the door opens, and there is the starter.

"Listen, Tony," he says sternly. "What did you do to the chinchillas?"

An elderly man and woman stand to the side. The cross-eyed old man holds a small wooden cage. One of the slats is broken, and a pointy-nosed chinchilla sticks its head out, greedily sniffing the old man's fingers, while its mate sleeps rolled up in a little ball, perfectly calm. The old lady stares at Garšva as though he had tried to murder her grandchildren.

"They say that up on the eighteenth you slammed the

door shut too quickly, shattered the cage, and almost killed the chinchillas!"

"That's right, O'Casey, I damaged the cage, because this gentleman entered the elevator and then, inexplicably, turned around and tried to exit. At that moment the door closed and the cage suffered some damage. The chinchillas, I believe, are fine, though the fellow got a little spooked. But his beloved is sleeping quite peacefully. It seems that, like most men, he's the more anxious one."

The starter smiled faintly. "OK, Tony. Go around the corner, and come back after these people have cleared out."

Walking away, Garšva hears the starter's words:

"He'll present himself to the manager and will be punished. What a criminal! The poor little creatures!"

Garšva comes back and the starter says:

"Bloody chinchillas! They belong in hell. Be careful, Tony."

"Thanks, O'Casey. I will."

The express from the tenth to the eighteenth. Your floor, here we are, please, thank you, button, hand to handle, going up. I'm not angry that the old people lodged a complaint. I was inattentive. Who told me to dream about the Valley of Josaphat? Poor, sweet old people. They're probably childless and will raise those chinchillas like their dearest darlings. Maybe I should follow their example, maybe that would save me?

Elena and I – together. Domestic bliss. A little house somewhere in Jamaica. We have a whole floor to ourselves. We hang some reproductions. We arrange our books. The art books and poets look serious. A separate little shelf for our own people. In the evenings we listen to music, read, and argue mildly, savouring it. The lamp shines, and it has a green glass shade. We find Station C, it doesn't have marble columns, but its vestibule offers peace. And on the coffee table – fresh flowers. And our faces always contain the possibility of smiles. And our dreams – a sense of awakening. And our embraces – the first trip to Jones Beach. And our emblem is the dead noblemen's heads. We play at leisure. We stack blocks, build castles, dream about life and death. And the books offer us some help. Not only Homer or Dante. Our own authors too. We drink sparkling wine and a flamingo flares up on the expensive ebony table; we sail on Lake Lucerne, and, in that other land, a dead boy plays a tune on the guitar that has never been heard on this earth. And the rising sun once again awakens our world, and we live in the cool, endless North with field, path, meadow, cross. Palms, my beloved palms, sing slender in this windy oasis.

Zoori, zoori, magical word, magical key, magical desire, magical conventionality, magical nostalgia, nostalgia for an unbreakable cage.

And then one day, in our little cage, a child is born.

Chapter 9

From Antanas Garšva's Notebooks

My earliest memories are not dramatic. But they are more vivid and indelible than others that came later and would normally be considered more important. My childhood memories are like those African masks: thick lips, holes for eyes, hypnotic facial relief.

It's nonsense, of course, to think that my first memory is authentic. It was probably shaped by knowledge acquired later. But today I still believe that I suddenly sensed in the absolute darkness that I existed – without body, space or time. All I had was an abstract sense of myself. As though I were more primitive than an amoeba. As though I were God, hovering in black non-existence before the creation of the universe.

Next there is Karlsbad, a man, a bunch of cherries. Our family spent one summer at that Austrian resort before the First World War. My mother was dissolving her kidney stones in the mineral baths. I have only a vague memory of Karlsbad. My parents bought a lot of coloured postcards and, when showing them to me later, would tell me where we had been and what we had done. And it would seem to me that I could see a vaulted hall, women with pinched waists and enormous hats, blue lake water and little red boats and the cone-shaped, snowy mountains. Even these memories are like the conception of the amoeba or God. But the trip on the funicular is real and indisputable.

We were climbing upward. I was sitting in the cable car by the window. I remember the lace on my mother's cuffs, my father's pointy moustache, the crooked, backward-leaning fir trees. And the station and the wagon in front of us. A man was leaning out the window. The man's face was red, and he was eating cherries of the same colour. I was looking at the cherries and the man was looking at me. Then, reaching out the window, he offered me two cherries and said something. The cherries gleamed in the sunlight. I took them. The cable cars separated. The man's rattled downward, ours groaned on upward. Two sticky, round, red cherries, which it seemed a pity to eat, lay in my palm. I put them in my mouth and then took them out again.

"Eat them," said my mother. I didn't dare, and rolled them in my palms. The cherries were beautiful, so I wanted to look at them. The cherries were sweet, so I wanted to eat them.

I can't remember the fate of those cherries. I remember my sticky fingers, the cherries softening, a vague resignation.

Then the waiting crashed in. I was eight years old. Our house stood at the edge of the small town, close to a marsh. Hummocks and crooked birches; a spruce forest on the horizon; the mournful cries of lapwings; the mist, which even the midsummer sun couldn't dissolve. The mist hung over the quagmire, and the frogs, the lapwings and the grasses glimmered, as though reflected in hundred-year-old mirrors. Were you to see Cinderella amongst these pools of water, you wouldn't be surprised. Cinderella – in her smoky rags, a basket in her hand, an expression that reveals she is searching for her prince, her red slippers muddy from the marsh.

My father had decided that he knew how to plaster walls. Of course, the rough plaster soon dried up, cracked and fell to the floor in geometric shapes. These uneven triangles, squares and rectangles were my favourite toys, which I used to build a castle for my own Cinderella. My parents, both high school teachers, would leave me in the locked, empty flat. I didn't attend school and did my lessons at home. At the time I was weak and often got dizzy, so I wasn't allowed to go outside on my own.

Waiting would soon arrive. It would stand next to me, like a concerned stepmother. Cold, strict, righteous, inflexible.

And here is a path. A pebbly path through the windless marsh. The wind never disturbs the crown of the spruce forest. I can see my foreshortened body in the marsh water. The hair falling to my shoulders. A golden chain around my neck. Cinderella walking next to me. I'm leading her to the unfinished castle which I built from my father's rough plaster. In Cinderella's basket – a single rose. Why? Roses don't grow in marshes. There, past the spruce forest, another world, another sky. Fragrant, gentle, somnolent. Surrounded by thick walls, where armed guards stand ready to hurl their lances. But the lances will be lowered, the gates will open and Cinderella will lead me inside. And there needn't be very much inside. Reddish painted floors; cracks; a crawling spider – a wise inhabitant of the unfinished castle. He knows why the rose is scented, why Cinderella's gait makes the guards reverently lower their lances and kneel.

But… Waiting was standing right there. Suddenly I could see the room in which I was playing. The pieces of plaster arranged in a semicircle. The green painting on the wall, a gift from my father's pupils. In copying a postcard the artist had made the mistake of erasing the circle that had been so carefully sketched with a No. 1 pencil around the setting sun. I could see the table legs, a twig wedged under one of them. I could see the hole in the sofa, the sawdust escaping from it. I could see my dirty nails. I picked my nose. I wanted to cry, to laugh. I was overwhelmed by waiting for my parents, who wouldn't be home soon.

Then I would decide to fight. To chase away that anxious feeling of waiting. To frighten it. To destroy it. To make it laugh. And I would open the window, hear the lapwing cries and draw the menacing dampness into my lungs.

I was an Indian. Brave and ruthless. My hands clutched my enemies' bloody scalps. Waiting was forced to clamber out the open window.

I was a knight. My double-edged sword would slice through the ceiling, shatter the light bulb, slash the sofa. Waiting would be hacked into pieces.

I was a cannibal. Huge cauldrons hissed, white men boiling in them. The room hummed from fire and the smoke. Waiting would be burnt up or choked.

I was a circus clown. I did somersaults, and fell flat on the ground. Laughed with a crazy voice. Waiting would have to cheer up.

And, eventually, I would get tired. Once again I was sitting by the scattered pieces of plaster. The spider and the castle guards have hidden in the cracks in the floor. Cinderella... is gone. There is no other world, no other sky, that is fragrant, gentle, sleepy. Waiting was still standing right there. A concerned stepmother. I would close the window. I didn't want to listen to the lapwings, didn't want to breathe the damp air. Once again I was staring at the table legs, the painting, the sawdust, the green lamp, the wispy clouds. An indistinct tune buzzed in my ear. Perhaps that was the birth of the sound that would become the word *zoori!*

I waited for my parents, my heart pounding. It gradually got darker. Sky and objects turned grey. I no longer resisted Waiting. I sat on the floor, picking my nose. I might have screamed if I had sensed that Waiting was no longer there. Sounds from the town bounced off the windowpanes. A locomotive hooted, truck wheels rattled, church bells peeled. My boyish heart pounded. Louder than the sounds of the waning evening.

My parents would arrive unexpectedly. That's what happens, when you're waiting so hard. At first they seemed to ignore me, were busy with their coats, the sentences they had brought in from the street, the lamp, dinner. Shoes fell to the floor and were replaced by slippers, kindling was split, the wood stove began to hiss, and as everything calmed down, I became lonely. Completely alone, as even Waiting had left. Where had it gone? Had it sneaked out through the door and sunk to the bottom of the marsh? Had it slipped in between the floorboards? Could it have curled up into the round sun in the student's painting? And I was sad that I had lost my stepmother. And I couldn't understand this contradiction. I had waited anxiously for my parents and was disappointed when they arrived. And I remained silent when my father noticed the scattered pieces of plaster and scolded me for being slovenly, and I was weak because I was lazy, didn't respect my father's work, and should be apprenticed to a shoemaker, as God often punishes people with such brats.

Cinderella with a basket in her hand, and in the basket a rose. I had to face arithmetic exercises and my stern father at the other end of the table. Another world? A dirty, awkward nakedness. *Zoori*, where is the melody? I can't hear it. Will I ever hear it?

Later still, I saw the tree. I was sixteen. We were on a summer holiday in Palanga. Laughing, my friend Aldona tossed my bamboo cane into the narrow Ronžė river. She added that I am thinner than the stick and have teeth like an ichthyosaur.

That afternoon I was walking alone on the beach near some fishermen's boats. They smelt of tar and fish. I stopped and dug into the sand with the tip of my shoe. The calm sea rippled nearby. Small waves separated me from the white glow. I wanted to leave the shore and walk into the sea. Like Christ. Just a few steps separated me from becoming a miracle. I knew that a miracle is reality turned into perfection. Like a leap into the air. I couldn't jump higher than one metre sixty. Even on my best form, I couldn't jump higher than one metre fifty-seven. I couldn't walk on the sea; I could only drown in it or look at it, and I was afraid of drowning.

So I continued to look at the sea. Sailboats glided on the horizon. Could I plant a mast with a faded canvas and sail away, gripping the wheel firmly? I breathed in the smell of tar and fish, and turned the sand with the tip of my shoe.

Suddenly, my whole being shivered in ecstasy. It seemed to me that I was stretching upward, that my head was higher that the pines on Swedes' Hill. I could hold the sun in my hands, and... how silly to want only to walk on the sea! When one could uproot trees and throw them around, causing the inhabitants of Swedish ports to wonder why they were covered in pine needles. Or hang the chapel on Birutė's Hill up in Heaven. I could fish out my bamboo stick, a Chaldean sorcerer's wand, and sketch magical symbols in the air. Let the stars shine during the day, let the stars sing and worship me as the most powerful of all. Great miracles aren't necessary. For I can contain limitless power and joy within myself!

I can't remember everything I got up to on the seashore by the fishermen's boats. I sang a toreador's aria in a false baritone, my leg thrust proudly forward, the high "so" of my tremulous howl softened by the monotonous murmur of the sea.

I danced an improvised dance. It was a priestess's prayer to Kastytis and Jūratė as they made love in their castle beneath the sea.[65] My long legs dug up the sand, I squatted

65   In the well-known Lithuanian legend, the sea princess Jūratė falls in love with the young fisherman Kastytis, who has disturbed the peace in her underwater kingdom. The love between a goddess and a mortal evokes the wrath of the god of thunder and lightning, Perkūnas, who in his fury shatters Jūratė's amber castle, which explains why small pieces of amber wash on to the shores of the Baltic after a storm.

down, grasping them, swaying my behind, showing the whites of my eyes.

I even gave a speech to the masses, the words mere symbols of something incredibly important.

"As you know... it is everything... let us stoke the fire, long live... raise and rise up... all... upward... I will show you the way to the magical light, I, I, ..."

And I shook the hands of all those greeting me, smiled charmingly, and leapt up as the crowd raised me on their arms and carried me, shouting, "It is him! It is him! He is ours!"

And then another sensation joined ecstasy and irritatingly penetrated my body, and my magnificence faded, like the foam of the waves dissolves in the sand. As though my eyes had just been opened. Here is a fisherman's boat. Further on, some blackened shells. Ahead – the grey sea. The skinny pines on Swedes' Hill . The empty seashore disappears around a bend. I understood. I needed to piss. That's what shattered my ecstasy. I leant against the edge of a boat. And felt relief from having held it in so long. And, just as the sand drank up my urine like foam from a wave, I heard a rustling. I turned my head. Damn! I'd forgotten to look in the direction of Birutė's Hill. The woman was right there. Very tanned in a bright red bathing suit, an orange robe hanging off her shoulder. She had probably seen and heard my idiotic song, and dance, and speech, and how I now stood contorted by the boat.

The woman walked past me – a screaming blemish in a grey world. I burst into tears of shame and walked home on the sand. The magical world evaporated. What ridiculously long legs! And teeth like an ichthyosaur's! And my own stench! What an idiot!

An empty pedestrian bridge lay ahead, like a corroded poker frozen in a puddle. The seaweed washed up by the Baltic reeked, and the rain began to pour, and the dwarf pines murmured. I walked along the streets of the resort. The gravel crackled, my nose was cold and my back itched.

There's the villa where Aldona is staying. The silliest girl in Palanga. Who cares if she has breasts and can wiggle her bum? I decided not to think about it any more.

That evening I lay in bed, looking through the window. It had stopped raining. I saw a tree and two stars. I had calmed down. My fingers wandered around the blanket.

Stars wandering around the blanket. Like two spiders. Both have five legs. The stars wander around on the dark blanket. Legs pressed together, flexible bones, the stars make love or war. A tree stood there, cut out of black tin. I felt it. My toes are cold. I turned towards the wall. The day's fragments formed a lump in my throat. I shouldn't have gazed so longingly at that useless girl. And why did I give her that lovely bamboo cane, like a prince bestowing a gift on Cinderella? Aldona is no Cinderella. Her father has an important job in the Finance Ministry, she'll marry a Kurhauzas regular.[66]

An acute shame washed over me. I curled my toes. That scene on the beach! What impotent grandeur! The tree and the two stars stood out beyond the window.

An impenetrable tin mass. My room is tight. And I am a tiny wad about to be crushed by the encroaching walls. Medieval times are approaching. I've been locked up in a torture chamber whose walls will come together. They'll crush me slowly, so as to prolong my writhing. The world was retreating, the tin walls closing in.

I leapt out of bed and ran to the window. Thank God – the tin mass was only a tree! I could see its individual leaves. And the many stars in the sky. The sea whispered faintly. I could hear my father snoring in the next room. I walked barefoot around the several square metres and the space felt as enormous as the entire universe. I felt young and strong.

Hey, I'm a good football player, I swim, and though my arms aren't the strongest I've knocked out two enemies. I'm fast. They say that my poems aren't bad, that they should

66 The first and main hotel and restaurant in Palanga at that
     time.

be submitted to the high school students' journal. Away with Medieval times! Away with Aldona and the mouldy Ronžė brook! It feels good to walk barefoot, at night. Tomorrow I'll try diving from five metres. From three my dive is perfection, but tomorrow I know it'll be even more perfect from five. A miracle will happen tomorrow. I lay down and quickly fell asleep.

*

The long break. From 8:30 to 9:15. Garšva and Stanley go together.

"Cafeteria?" asks Garšva.

"First, the basement," replies Stanley.

"Why?"

"You'll see."

"You'll unlock your locker?"

"You're so boring, Tony."

The two of them wait for the "back" elevator. The starter here sways side to side, he had polio as a child.

"Ten years in the hotel," says Stanley.

"That he's been swaying there?"

"And he likes overtime. His wife works in the kitchen. Her lover is Puerto Rican. They avoid overtime."

The paralysed starter gives them a friendly wink.

"You'll get an elevator soon, guys."

"He has a nice face," notes Stanley.

"His wife's is nice too," he adds, watching the elevator arrows.

Some old chairs are stacked at the end of the corridor. Suddenly one chair falls down noisily because the lobby doors are opened wide. Two burly hotel detectives drag in an unconscious guest. He is old, his legs drag along the floor, his eyeballs have rolled up into his eyelids, the whites shining like matt lampshades. His mouth hangs open, saliva drips through his false teeth. A woman dressed in black, with a rosy, idiotic face, walks behind. Her shoes are scuffed, her white cuffs grimy, her old-fashioned hat has faded to brown. She holds a clear bag of walnuts in one hand, and three nuts in the other.

"They're his," she says.

"The tenth, quick," says one of the detectives. The starter sways towards the control box and presses all the buttons.

"Take them, sir," says the woman, offering the unconscious man the bag of nuts.

"I have a feeling the gentleman isn't interested in nuts right now," says Stanley politely.

"They're his nuts. He was walking through the lobby, holding them in his hand. Then he collapsed. I picked up the bag and three nuts fell out. I picked them up," explained the woman, holding the three nuts under Stanley's nose.

"Looks pretty dead," notices the second detective, squeezing he old man's hand.

"The doctor just got to the tenth," the starter announces. The old man unexpectedly wheezes.

"Look – he's alive!" exclaims the second detective.

"Not for long. I've seen a lot of these deaths," explains his friend.

The elevator arrives with a whir and within seconds the three passengers disappear.

"Mister! Mister! Your nuts! You forgot your nuts!" the woman shouts desperately, even though the elevator lights already indicate the sixth floor.

"You're free to eat them. Or give them to your kids," suggests Stanley. And the two of them get into an elevator headed for the basement.

Ten minutes later Garšva and Stanley are holding trays in the hotel staff cafeteria. The toothless Puerto Rican is clanging plates. Cauldrons steam with yesterday's food the hotel guests didn't finish.

"Leftover turkey?"

"Sure."

"And a glass of milk?"

"Sure."

"Rice?"

"Sure."

"You're really chatty today, Tony. The old man with the nuts?"

"Maybe."

"Oh, I see."

The cafeteria is on the second floor. It is long and narrow, with wide windows looking on to 34th. Red, white, green and blue neon lights illuminate the faces of the seated – to economise the cafeteria is lit with weak bulbs. The same red paint as in the rest of the hotel, only here it's dirtier and sadder. The walls once had paintings, reproductions of vague landscapes, but then they were suddenly taken down. The new assistant manager decided that the reproductions were outdated. The assistant had visited the Museum of Modern Art, and promised to find some more modern ones. But he lasted only a month. The hotel administration fired the modern assistant when they discovered that he was an exhibitionist who liked to show off in subway stations. And so new reproductions were never hung in the cafeteria. Faded squares remain on the walls, like the imaginary clothes in the story of the naked king.

Garšva and Stanley sit down by a window. They stare at the street as they eat. Their heads are spinning. There's an empty bottle of Seagram's in Stanley's locker. Other lunchers chatter away at the surrounding tables. Bellboys in unbuttoned red jackets, kitchen staff with stained aprons, office clerks getting their caffeine fixes and a woman photographer with a face painted so heavily that even she isn't sure of her age.

A foursome of black kitchen maids sits nearby, each sentence followed by shrieks of laughter from a recent joke.

"When de golden trumpets sound
Where will yo' soul be found?
Standin' aroun', standin' around
When de golden trumpets sound,"

says Garšva, chewing his turkey leftovers.

"Negro songs?"

"Yeah."

"You're still a fan," Stanley notes, drinking his milk. Garšva stops chewing.

"Why?"

"I felt the same way when I first heard Mozart.

"And now?"

Stanley's eyes are almost swollen shut.

"Now all that remains is the knowledge that such music exists."

"You don't listen to Mozart any more?" The eyes are revealed, a film of red. Stanley's face is painted red by the neon lights.

"Yeah. Concerto in B-flat Major. Fantastic larghetto. Italian opera arias can kill you with their painful beauty. Concerto in D Major for violin. The rondo is graceful, like my mother dancing the mazurka. Did you know that my mother still dances the mazurka at Polish parties? And well, they say. Yeah. The *Haffner* Symphony. Allegro con spirito, I think. A devil in a wig is about to bow, an invitation to a minuet. Yeah. I don't even listen to the *Requiem* any more. Because, like Mozart, I'm at death's door. I listen to what the Seagram's tells me. Seven Crown, I think."

The black women are still cackling after every sentence. When de golden trumpets sound. Around, around, around, around. The woman photographer chews slowly. Her facial features don't move. A stocky bellhop laughs loudly.

"Just imagine! Four suitcases, like they were filled with rocks, and just a quarter. And I even explained the subway system to the guy. How to find Halsey Street. And that Eisenhower had lunch in the hotel next door yesterday. And some other stuff. A quarter! The guy had a camel-hair coat!"

Golden around. On the wall, one of the faded squares is painted by the flash of a faded advertising star. A Renoir is reborn and dies. The trumpet of art. Two Puerto Ricans enter the cafeteria. They chatter away in Spanish, waving their hands. The glasses of orange juice they carry don't spill. A laughing black woman's belly jiggles. "They're fast!" she shrieks. And the chorus agrees. A black Greek chorus on a smaller scale. Aroun' aroun' aroun'. The "ahs" and "ohs" echo, muffled, like in a steamy jungle after heavy rain. Cars drive down the street, a jaundiced clerk stares at his empty coffee cup, the boss's muted calls echo from the main-floor lobby, but it's impossible to know who he's calling and why. Aroun' aroun' aroun' aroun'.

"What are you muttering?" asks Stanley.

"Around," replies Garšva.

"You're done for."

"I've known that for twenty years."

"I meant that one day, you'll be done for."

"Everyone's done for one day. Night. Morning. Evening."

"Wise words. You look like you're trying to decide something."

"And you?"

"The Socratic method?"

Garšva observes Stanley. A Mozart fan, and he's even heard of Socrates. A long drunken *šlėkltelė's* face. And shaking hands.

"Listen, Stanley. Why do you…"

"You want to know why I work here? It's temporary. I'm going to kill myself. *Zasvistali – pojechali.*"[67]

Garšva doesn't dare ask why. He drinks his milk and watches the Renoir appear and disappear. The black women have stopped laughing. They lean their heads together, whispering like conspirators. They're planning to murder a rich widow. When she falls asleep, two of them will stand watch in the hallway while the other two smother the widow with pillows. Then they'll grab her jewels and all four will hide out in Harlem. They'll repent in a black prophet's

---

67 *Zasvistali – pojechali*: We whistle – we go (Polish). Stanley's Polish is poor, so some of his expressions do not make sense.

apartment as the horns scream and the drums roll. What nonsense! The black women are probably gossiping about their girlfriends or complaining about guests.

"Thomas Wolfe spends several pages describing a man who landed on the street from some floors up," says Garšva.

"Literature makes everything beautiful. Even ugly things. Suicide is ugly. But I need to do it."

"Why?"

"I can't give you a good reason. I went to high school. Studied piano. And started to drink. Why? Maybe you can tell me. You're a European, you have all the traditional answers."

"You're not being completely frank," Garšva concludes.

Stanley looks at him as though he were a student trying to explain why he hasn't done his homework.

"I am being frank. I really want to kill myself. *Dziękuję.*"[68]

"Then what are you waiting for?" asks Garšva, now somewhat alarmed because Stanley's face becomes grave. There is something intangibly fine about his features. It could be a past pride, a nobleman's sword, an ambitious narrowing of the lips, a multicoloured garment, an embroidered sash and *konfederatka.*[69]

"*Idz srač,*" says Stanley, and he gets up and leaves.[70] Garšva cringes. I didn't want to upset him, all I did was ask. Maybe I'm like the old lady who offered a dying man some nuts? Could the faded squares from the reproductions hold the answer? Stanley's soul is a faded square, and Mozart will fade away when the snack bar's neon lights go out. And the black women won't whisper as they clean rooms. And the jaundiced clerk is already counting on the other side of the partition. And I still have twenty-eight minutes. Truly I didn't want to insult Stanley. There's no answer to my question. The answer will be articulated by theologians,

---

68   *Dziękuję*: Thank you (Polish).

69   *konfederatka*: a traditional, four-pointed Polish military hat.

70   *Idz srac*: Go and shit yourself (Polish).

114

psychologists, sociologists, moralists, authors of theses. One must act this way. It had to be this way, so it wouldn't be that way. Or that way, this way.

The black women have already left. The woman photographer, a twentieth-century Veronika, stubs out her cigarette in an ashtray.[71] The Puerto Ricans have disappeared. The cafeteria empties out. The golden trumpets no longer sound. Aroun'? Aukštoji Panemunė is all around. The *vėlės* have climbed down from their high benches and now surround me. I can't make out their shapes. Everything is mixed up. Gnarled tree roots, the misty, swaying marsh, a wooden Christ standing on a sinking hummock; are those tears on His carved features, did this fine rain sprinkle down from Heaven? A harpsichord? It could be a harpsichord. Why wouldn't a *vėlė* play the harpsichord? *Vėlės* aren't concerned with clothes or historical periods. There are words. Magical words. Dead noblemen's sculptural eyes, and brass snakes slithering through the rusted ring of a door handle. And a choir of *kaukai*, field and harvest gods.

> *Dumbluoja dienelė,*
> *Dumbluoja giedrioji*
> *In vakarą, vakarėlį.*
>
> *Oi, leidžias saulelė*
> *Tamsiuosna debesysna*
> *Už žalių girelių.*[72]

---

71 Veronika: a jilted young woman in a short story by the Lithuanian author Antanas Vienuolis (1882–1957).

72 Lithuanian folk song:
The day darkens,
The brightness darkens
In the evening, the evening.
Oh, the sun is setting
into the dark clouds
beyond the green woods.
And the clouds are glooming
Over the green wood.

Would it be blasphemy if Christ patted a *kaukas* on the back and turned the marsh water to red wine? Or a fairy dried His rain-soaked face with her braids? I think this could be one solution. A solution? Could this be the beginning of the poem I've been waiting for so long?

But why do I hear the black Greek choir nearby? The black women's laughter – jungle drumming. The black women's laughter – Elena's fist pounding on the locked door. Lord, oh my Lord, who art inside me, I love her! All I can do is repeat the tired words. I love, love, love, love her! I love her, Elena. Stanley, where are you? Stanley, can't you see that I'm as sentimental as an old maid? But I won't jump out of a window. I'm afraid to die, Stanley.

Chapter 10

The Chagall reproduction was unchanged. A cloud-haired woman flew over a Russian town. And another, a green bouquet in her hand, fell from her waist. A blurry sleigh glided by, a man waving a whip. The walls were still stamped with ornaments, possibly Roman. Books both arranged neatly on shelves and scattered on the table. Thick with dust. An expensive album lay open, and a splayed Soutine child soared over the page like a little cardboard man pulled by a string. Next to it sat two glasses with murky dregs, an abandoned cherry in one, an ashtray full of cigarette butts, a purse. Articles of men's and women's clothing and underwear were piled on the lone armchair. A wrinkled sheet slipped off the green sofa, a quilt in a bluish cover lay on the flowery linoleum.

"I will give you a carnelian ring and an abandoned streetcar in Queens Plaza," said Garšva. He kissed the mole in the bend of her neck.

"I'll take the ring to a jeweller tomorrow. He'll adjust it to fit your finger. We'll go to see the streetcar wagon next Tuesday. I'm free on Tuesday."

Elena licked her parched lips.

"Are you thirsty?" asked Garšva.

"I want. Some water."

He got up and found his blue robe. His back muscles tensed briefly. When he returned from the kitchen with the water, Elena said, "I knew that you were lying on the sand next to me, and I could see your back. I so wanted to touch it."

As she drank the water, Garšva picked up the bottle of

White Horse from the floor and poured himself a third of a glass.

"You drink it straight?"

"Yes."

"He drank the scotch in one swig. He sat down on the sofa next to her legs. He stroked their skin, its fine golden stubble."

"Just lie there, lie there," he said when Elena startled. "Just lie there."

It was a foggy day.

"Lie there, that's it."

He kissed her ankles.

"Cover me, I'm a little cold."

He covered her with the quilt, and she smiled faintly. Small, even, bluish teeth.

"I lied. I was waiting for you yesterday. I saw you. You were standing by the drugstore. Mine is the corner window." And she added, "There's a lot of blue in your room. The robe, the quilt cover, the book spines, the clock, the linoleum. Do you like blue?"

"I like the bluish veins on your legs," said Garšva.

"Don't play games. You're very young, and I got tired. My head is empty, like a nobleman's."

"Like a nobleman's?"

"My own inner noblewoman wanted to hear some harpsichord. My husband mocks me, you know. I bought all these harpsichord records."

Garšva took the bottle.

"Shall I pour you some?"

"A little. Into my water."

They drank in silence.

"I don't want you to mock me. Be quiet. I've read your poems. I asked my husband to take you to Jones Beach. I knew that you two had met at the Vaineikis's. I knew, in advance – yes – that you would be mine. Cold calculation, you're thinking? Don't speak. Trust me, I don't know, I really don't know. It's true that I foresaw some of this. The drink is warming me up. No, don't kiss me right now. Why did you buy it? Do you need artificial love? Be quiet. Drink, if you want. And pour me some. That's enough."

And they both drank.

"My head is spinning. What's the difference? Real, artificial... I'm just a former high school teacher. And I loved Vilnius. I used to walk for hours. One fall, you know those popular books about metempsychosis, well it seems I've already experienced it many times. If you like I can tell you about it, didn't you ask me to? About the dead noblemen's heads? Fine. Listen. One night, a handsome young man was walking down Pylimo Street. His collar was turned up, a biting wind blew, it was autumn, he was rushing home after his classes, do you know the columns in the university courtyard? Don't laugh. You're the poet. A young dreamer leans against each one of the columns, the ends of his necktie flutter, dry leaves rustle, he's reciting verse. Be quiet. I really wanted to cry, yesterday, in the square. It's been a long time since I've cried. I feel good here. Listen. I'll continue. And if it isn't interesting, cut me off. No, don't kiss me. A good-looking young man, fair-haired, a few freckles around his nose, don't smile, that's how I imagine it, and hungry, because he isn't well off, so what if that's cliché, the whole story happened under the Germans, the young man was in a rush, it was close to curfew. Near the house with the sculptures of noblemen's heads in the cornices he heard a harpsichord playing. Naturally, he came to a stop, it was unusual to hear harpsichord music under the Germans. The doors to that building are heavy, copper lion heads with chains in their jaws, and the handsome young man didn't dare touch the chain. And then the doors opened on their own, and it was dark inside, a greenish light shone from above. The young man climbed up the granite stairs. The light became brighter, as did the sound of the harpsichord. On the upper landing, gold-plated statues held torches, they burned with greenish flames. And at the turn, a red carpet led towards the hall. No, don't give me more to drink. Sit still. The young man entered the hall. Many candles burned in malachite candlesticks; fat cherubim blew on long pipes: white grapes, apples and pears in woven baskets; and the candle flames rose, unmoving, even though the fair young man felt a breeze on his back. Don't smile, that's how I imagined it. Imagined it logically. The main doors were open, do you see? Some people stood there, unmoving, in the hall, with dark clothes, pointy beards, white ruffles, white faces, eyeless, because of the shadows that fell on their eyelids. I think that the sculptures of noblemen's heads had been placed atop velvet clothes. They stood respectfully, their heads bowed. And... listen. In the hall, by the wall, a greenish harpsichord – strange, isn't it, because candle flames are normally a clear yellow? And a woman sat playing, in a white gown, lace trailing on the parquet that had been polished to shine like a mirror. Only her waxen fingers moved. Her long fingers travelled the keyboard. Two red servants supported a blind man who listened, seemingly content, as he was smiling. You're curious to know what the pianist's face looked like? I don't know. Once I imagined my own face there. Don't laugh, I powdered it and looked at myself in the mirror. Then I decided: that's me. But it doesn't really matter what her face looked like. She noticed the fair young man and raised her hands from the keys. And naturally, he approached her, knelt, and kissed her outstretched hand. You can kiss me now, if you like. That's enough. Later, my dear. Just sit and listen. The fair young man invited the white-gowned woman to dance. The two red servants gently helped the blind man on to the stool and he began to play a minuet. He nodded his head, probably enjoying himself. And the noblemen's heads swayed to the dancers' rhythm. And everything was reflected in the polished parquet. And...

no, let me cry, they're childish tears. The gilded statues stepped off their pedestals, you remember – the statues from the upper landing? They entered the hall, the greenish light from the lanterns washed over everything, and the chains hung from their necks, the chains wrenched from the lions. Fine. Pour me a little. Thank you. That's enough. And then the fair young man saw: he was embracing a dead tree trunk. And around him, in a semicircle, stood more headless trunks. Around the rotted harpsichord. And the cherubim, and their pipes, and the baskets of fruits – everything was thick with mould. The candles went out. The torches burned. Where did the blind man and his red servants go? I don't know. Mice scratched around in the splintered remains of the parquet floor. The fair young man let go of the black trunk. It fell down, the echo of its fall repeating itself several times. And as the fair young man ran down the stairs, he heard someone pounding on the harpsichord. The instrument shrieked, as though it were being immolated. When the young man found himself back on the street, the doors closed. The moon shone, the noblemen's heads hung from the cornices. Now I'll explain it to you. I didn't make all of it up. There was an old Polish woman who lived in Vilnius, half mad, destitute among her books and candles. Like the last of the witches. A bit of bacon, butter and Polish conversation would put her in a good mood. We had a long talk. About the harpsichord. Now come to me."

Garšva pulled back the quilt, slipped off his robe, and lay down next to her. Elena's fingers wandered over his body.

"Do you want to know what happened to the handsome young man?"

"Yes?"

"The next morning he went back to the building. He found the guard and was let in. The building had been closed for many years. He found everything as he had seen it, when he had run out. The wooden trunks were some folk sculptor's unfinished gods. Nobody knew why he hadn't completed them. And..."

"And?"

"I'm lying. The old Polish woman told me this story. I went to see that building. And tried to play the rotted harpsichord. Dissonant sounds. Dust. Cold. The gilded statues were in fairly good shape. Did you like this story?"

"She gets herself excited with these kinds of stories. Hoffmann resurrected in service of Eros," thought Garšva, and said, "I remembered my mother."

"Make love to me," Elena said.

And again there were only the Chagall reproduction, the tidy and scattered books, the ashtray full of cigarette butts, the purse, the pile of clothes, the floating Soutine child, the wrinkled sheet, two glasses on the linoleum, and next to them a tangled quilt in a blue cover.

*

Stanley comes back with two cups of coffee.

"I'm very sorry," they say simultaneously, smiling guiltily.

"Drink your coffee," says Stanley, pushing one of the cups forward.

"I didn't want to upset you, Stanley," says Garšva.

"You see, I ask myself a lot of questions too. I'm a writer, you know. I'm glad you came back."

"Drink your coffee," is all Stanley can mumble. Then, after a silence, says, "My father once said to me that Poles are quite a hot-headed people. I believe him. He used to beat me, would still like to. And I would love to beat up some of our guests. On the whole I promise not to swear in Polish, but you'll allow me to in English, I hope?"

"Go for it."

"OK, Tony."

"OK."

They drink their coffee.

"You want to know what I'm waiting for?" Stanley asks suddenly, looking Garšva in the eyes.

"Not necessarily."

"You're polite. I have a girlfriend. The same one with the sunken belly button. *Kocham*.[73] Get it?"

"Absolutely. Because… I have a girlfriend too."

"Aren't we a couple of odd guys. Maybe we're each other's doubles."

"There are a lot of doubles in the world. And they have girlfriends."

"Does yours love you?"

Garšva sips his coffee. Then mutters, "I've lost her."

"Why?"

"I gave her up."

"She's unfaithful?"

"I couldn't love her."

"Oh, so you…"

"Not that. I'm ill, Stanley. I fainted the last time. And I spoke to her husband. And promised him that I wouldn't sleep with her any more. And the last time she came to see me, I didn't let her in."

"You still love her?"

"Very much, Stanley."

"What's wrong with you?"

"I… really don't know. I once had my head split open. But even before that, when I was younger, I had seizures."

"You've been to a doctor?"

"Yes. He told me to come one more time. But I didn't."

"Fucking hell," curses Stanley, and drinks his coffee. He falls silent, then continues in a calm voice:

"I caught mine with some clerk from downtown. But I still love her; just like before."

Now even the bellboys have left. And the woman photographer. An elderly watchman sits in a corner eating noodles. The noodles are long and he swallows them like Goya's Saturn swallowing his children. The captain's low bass no longer echoes. It's quiet in the cafeteria. Like in a

---

73 *Kocham*: I love (Polish).

private apartment. The dirty red paint is even more vivid, so are the faded patches on the wall, the flickering advertising lights, and the cigarette butts, chewing gum wrappers and cigarette packages on the floor.

Kafka walks in the door. A sad Jew, his eyes full of knowledge: Jehovah wasn't willing to grant him an audience. Kafka's eyes say, "Why am I not Moses?" Oscar Wilde walks in the door, holding a sunflower. He looks around, as though this were the bank of the Seine and Dorian Gray's corpse were floating by. Baudelaire walks in the door. He observes the noodles slithering into the watchman's mouth. They are worms, and the worms are sucking on the man's gaping mouth. Rimbaud walks through the door. He reels, his arms full of guns, swords and daggers. A drunken boat slips from his embrace. An inebriated Verlaine walks in the door. "Which kind of poem would you like – religious or piquant?" he asks obsequiously, glancing at the coffee cups. Emily Dickinson walks in the door. Faded letters pinned to her white dress. She observes Garšva and Stanley closely and says: "So, my dear gentlemen, Elysium is as far away as the room next door." Ezra Pound walks in the door and says ironically, "Do you know what *Phanopoeia* is, and what are its parts? Rose white, yellow, silver; *saltus, concava vallis?*" And with the face of a wise Chinaman, Ezra Pound shouts "aoi! aoi!" Ženia walks in the door, accompanied by Nietzsche, who sings ecstatically, "I love you, Ariadne!" Garšva's mother walks in the door and looks at him for the last time.

Chapter 11

From Antanas Garšva's Notebooks

My mother was of noble birth. She had a coat of arms: an upright fish on a shield. But she did not like to talk about it, so I never learnt her precise genealogy. Except that she came from Telšiai.[74]

My mother was my first teacher (my father taught me arithmetic). And once again we were assisted by that green-globed lamp. The ragged book spines were my own fault: when I hadn't learnt a lesson I stretched out my answer by picking at them with my thin fingers. The notes of my mother's voice would fall round and gentle, and it seemed to me that, if I were to fall asleep listening to them, I would have a pleasant dream.

My mother liked black velvet dresses. They accentuated her slender waist, her full bust and hips. Her fingers would caress the tablecloth and once, hypnotised by the rhythmic strokes, I almost knocked over the inkwell. The chimes of the wall clock pressed up against my heart, while the textbook letters shimmered like the hieroglyphs of a lost land.

I remember my mother's lessons. They were the impressions of someone only briefly visiting Earth.

"The king put on his armour. The metalworkers had hammered lilies into it. The queen sobbed, and as her tears fell to the castle floor the mice and the ladies in waiting sobbed with her. The king rode off. And his squire rode off. And the knights. For another king lived in the next castle. And he too put on his armour. The metalworkers

---

74   Telšiai: a small city in western Lithuania.

125

had hammered lions on to it. The queen sobbed, and as her tears fell to the castle floor the mice and the ladies in waiting sobbed with her. The king rode off. And his squire rode off. And the knights. Two kings, two squires, and two armies met on the green plain. Both kings died in the bloody battle. And both squires. And the knights returned to their castles. And pledged their allegiance to each king's son, and vowed revenge. The queens raised the princes, the ladies in waiting – the squires, the mice – baby mice. That is the meaning of war, my son."

And later, in the same vein, my mother would review the key events and dates. I learnt of such men as Alexander the Great, Cyrus, Nero, Attila, Charles V. But they were all kings to me, their armour merely cast with other signs and years.

The lessons would end unexpectedly. My mother would close the books and pause to think for a moment. I waited for these pauses as though they were preludes to a miracle. The room, the furniture, the lamp would begin to glow. Every speck of dust, even a fly stain, was vivid and essential. Her hands, my grandmother's gold ring, which must never be removed. It would be like cutting off a finger.

And my mother's eyes would moisten. She would recite a poem. It could be a French poem, or German, Russian, or Lithuanian. This verse particularly struck me, for some reason:

> *Koenig ist der Hirtenknabe,*
> *gruener Huegel ist sein Thron,*
> *ueber seinem Haupt die Sonne*
> *ist die grosse gold'ne Kron!*[75]

The royal nature of history was likely responsible.

There was also someone called Muznierovski. I don't remember Muznierovski. Only my father's angry words.

---

75   From Heinrich Heine's poem, "The Shepherd Boy": "Here the shepherd is a king,/ His throne a grassy hill,/ The golden sun a wreath / Gracing his royal head."

"I know you like Polish men. A bow, a little hand, *smack, smack*, false compliments, glossy whiskers, courtly admiration. When in truth it's a transgression, a bed, a family destroyed. Muz-nie-rov-ski. You haven't forgotten?" My mother's eyes beseeched. My father didn't see me.

"You remember, eh? Muznierovski, eh? Muznierovskian whiskers? There I was, working twenty hours a day to support this family. I come home, and – sir and madam! *Panstwo*.[76] Did you do it with Muznierovski?" shrieked my father, and my heartbeat drowned out all the ticking clocks. Fistfuls of sharp-edged stones sank to the bottom of the murky pond. My father filled both of his pockets. In one sparkled diamonds, the other was heavy with rocks. And my mother would quietly leave the room. I tried to read a book, but its words merged with my father's. "…It was another era. People were different back then, they lived differently. With hair wax, hair wax, ax ax waxxxx. The land was more fertile, the forest full of game and fowl, and people were stronger, more vigorous. Muznie-rovski – did you do, doooooo it with him? Another youngster is sneering, *smack, smack*, hair wax, old people, who, enterprising…"

My eyes watered, my nose ran, I wiped it with my fist and the words in the book bulged as though I were reading through a magnifying glass.

"Go to bed!" my father would shriek, and I would shrink into a little ball.

The Muznierovski affair… Once, as I lay in bed, she crept in, white and calm, adjusted my blanket, and whispered:

"I loved someone, Antanukas. And left him. I stayed with your father. For you. For… the family. When you grow up, you'll understand me. And your father."

"I'll always love you, Mummy," I said.

"Keep loving me, my darling. But sleep now. Goodnight."

She never talked about it again, as much as I tried to persuade her to.

76 *Panstwo*: ladies and gentlemen (Polish).

Was the torture over Muznierovski the beginning of her illness? It's hard to say. A famous psychiatrist was certain that my mother had inherited schizophrenia. And that the end was inevitable. The tragedy was that my father didn't do anything when the illness first manifested itself.

I can no longer remember the precise date. That's what happens. My healthy mother became a future fantasy, my ill mother – the perpetual present.

At the time my father was playing Wieniawski variations for the German-language teacher. The teacher was a mature widow, stocky and bow-legged, with a nose like Goethe's and wiry black hair. Her oily skin glistened, so she reminded me of an old clothes brush. But somehow, she was prettier than my mother. I don't understand how it happened. What happened to the long oval face, the fair hair, the large, damp eyes, the thick eyelashes, the narrow waist, the full yet firm breasts? What happened to the fluid, relaxed gypsy movements, the soft blur at the edge of painted lips, the hypnotic fingers, each one following the last like galloping notes written by a composer in love with music. Long before, my father had brought home a large photograph of my mother and hung it on the wall. And my mother blushed, looked at my father with a strange expression, and then – for the first and last time in my presence – my father embraced her and kissed her on the lips.

Now she was a hag. The skin sagged. The forehead, cheeks and breasts drooped like wet underclothes. The thickened, callused lips. The sluggish body swayed heavily on swollen legs. The fair hair hung in witchlike tufts. Her neglected teeth – skull-like black holes.

And despite it all she tidied rooms, mended clothes, tried to kiss me at bedtime. Her speech deteriorated. She moved and worked like a convict who knows he will die in prison. Her imagination returned during her fits. These happened unexpectedly, so that each time my father and I thought it was the first time. At first they coincided with her periods, and some provincial doctor promised us that the fits would end when these ceased. Perhaps it was this promise, or perhaps residual sentiment, that held my father back from making a decision.

A fit. At first, a moment of lucidity. A lost gentleness reappeared in my mother's eyes. As though she felt a general relief. Like an old woman remembering her youth. We watched as she tried to say something amiable and searched for the necessary words. My father and I were frightened by this effort. We waited. It was coming, it would happen, now nothing could stop it.

"Fish. Beautiful fish. Silver," my mother would say, her fingers moving. An aged, heavy ballerina demonstrating that she had once been graceful. Her gaze pierced my father. With piercing insistence, so that he was forced to answer. My father tried to be casual.

"What kinds of fish, Mother?"

"Silver ones. Swimming. Remember?" My mother would give a restrained, mysterious snicker.

"I always said that she doesn't know how to make strawberry jam. The berries always fall apart. Not enough sugar. Am I right?"

"Absolutely, Mother," said my father colourlessly.

"Ha, ha. I'm right, I am, I am, ha, ha. Archangelsk isn't right either. It has to be Angelsk. There is only snow and lace there. Archangels' wings are like this."

My mother would stand and hold up her embroidery. She had been working on it for about two years. A dirty piece of cloth, small red crosses that failed to make a pattern. It was supposed to become a small tablecloth for a night table.

"That's right. That's what archangel wings are like," my father would hopelessly agree.

"You think so? You think so? Yes, yes?"

My mother stood, waiting for an answer. The answer would solve the mystery of the universe. She looked at my father as though he had risen from the dead and could see the afterlife.

"I'm sure of it," my father would reply. Suddenly my mother would calm down. And sit down. And would start speaking quite normally.

"Don't think that I don't know. I know everything. You play for the German-language teacher. You play, and she thinks that she is the first one you have ever played for. But you used to play for me. She's stupid, that German teacher of yours."

My mother would cackle, satisfied that she had won. The cruel prosecutor has hurled the strongest argument and the accused will be condemned, as the jury members are already thinking.

My father would jump up. He would automatically move towards the hanging violin, but then would turn away and go towards the door.

"You wait, wait, wait, wait! If you're leaving and I'm no longer yours, then take your clothes – they aren't mine, they aren't mine!"

Now I would press my fingers against my face. I couldn't watch this. And I couldn't run away either. My feet were nailed to the floor. I pressed my fingers against my face and heard the words.

"You stick your body into her body, stick it, stick it! Here, take them, take them!"

"Shut up, shut up!" my father shrieked.

I listened to the duet in red darkness. This is how people being seared with hot irons must sing. Lord, why was I so weak? Why couldn't I scream louder than they? Why couldn't I writhe on the floor? I was crushed by the horror of it. I could only release my fingers and watch.

My mother's dress and underclothes were scattered on the ground. I could see the little flowers on the dress, the pink camisole, the tangled stockings. The storm had blown over, ripped off the tattered clothes and thrown a short, black coat on to my mother. The coat had a little hook at the collar. She had worn it as a young woman. My mother held it closed with her hands. My ashen-faced father stood at the door. It was quiet. The curtain opened slowly on the last act.

This was the final scream. Of the last person on a dying Earth. And yet I could clearly see my mother's quivering double chin. The old prima donna was hitting the high note. My father's face would fill with blood. He would rush to the desk, pull out a nickel-plated revolver and trace the muzzle along his temple. As though using a razor. "I'll shoot myself, I'll shoot myself!" And my mother screamed. Tossing aside the revolver, my father would leap towards my mother, throw her on to the sofa and beat her with his fists. The coat would fall open and I would see my mother's naked, flabby body. And now she was no longer screaming but howling, like an animal being harmed. And then I would run outside to get help.

After that, everything happened in a blur. Neighbours trying to offer comfort; women dressing my mother; my father collapsed on the sofa; voices saying what a poor little boy I was.

But the violin still hung on the wall. And the apples and pears still lay on the dining table. And the linden trees grew by our house. They were fragrant in July. My friends played cops and robbers. Charlie Chaplin entertained the townspeople in the cinema and the priest sang in a strained baritone in the church. And I was looking at girls differently, reading, dreaming. I wanted to live. Like most people.

My father finally took action. I was the only one my mother trusted, so I was the one who executed the betrayal. I convinced her that we were going to Palanga for a summer holiday. She enjoyed the trip. Asked me a lot of questions. Went on and on about what a good son I was, how I should eat more because I was so thin. She asked me about school, books and friends. The two of us in the car, the driver had been warned, she was quiet, we were two lonely friends. She enjoyed the highway, the trees, the cottages, the woman with her buckets. She seemed perfectly normal. Towards evening we drove through some gates and stopped in front of a red-brick building marked Psychiatric Hospital.

The driver, orderlies and I were barely able to drag my mother out of the car. She didn't scream. She stared. Like the soul of someone recently deceased would stare upon discovering that all there was in the afterlife was hell.

And this expression of my mother's would haunt me whenever my teachers explained that the universe was created according to the principles of Good, Beauty and Harmony, and that man is guilty for his own misfortunes.

*

"I didn't call her on my day off," Stanley recounts.

"Yeah. I went to her house. The door was locked. I decided to wait in the street. And I waited for two or three hours. She came home arm in arm with that clerk. I knocked him out in a couple of minutes. And then slept with her. I caught the clerk with her again, in her room. He was dressed and managed to escape. And we slept together again. Wait! I'll remember in a second. *Psiakrew*. Did I pronounce it correctly?"[77]

"Yes."

"That's the blood of my ancestors speaking. I still go to see her. *Psiakrew*. You have no idea how good she is… you understand? *Kocham. Dziękuję.* Yeah."[78]

"And Mozart?"

"Mozart? I can't sit down to play. I want to rip out the keys and break the boards. Look – my hands are shaking. Once I got an offer to play the electric organ in a tavern. My father was sick, we needed the money. Have you ever heard one of those awful boxes? Playing requests on the electric organ. Bloody hell. Yeah. As though Bach or Handel had

77   *Psiakrew*: Bastard (Polish).
78   *Kocham*: I love (Polish). *Dziękuję*: Thank you (Polish).

gone mad. Working in a tavern you quickly learn to drink. Yeah. I never went back to Mozart. Right. If I didn't go back it must mean I wasn't made for Mozart."

"But Joe…"

"Joe? He started with Faust, but he'll finish in some nightclub. It would be great if it were a nice nightclub. Have you listened to the timbre of his voice, when he sings in the toilet? It's a miraculous squeaking. There's some hope."

"Fine, Stanley. But forgive me if I ask – why such a firm decision?"

"Why do I want to kill myself? I don't believe in anything any more. I can't do anything any more."

"You're a neurasthenic."

"Thanks. Like I said, we're a couple of neurasthenics."

"There are three of us."

"Who's the third?"

"The lady with the nuts." Stanley laughs. A youthful laugh, with white teeth.

"This city is going mad," thinks Garšva.

The writers are now leaving the cafeteria. Kafka stuffs his hands into the pockets of his extra long coat and walks out, stooped over. Oscar Wilde, waving his sunflower, also exits. Baudelaire once more glances at the watchman's plate. It's empty. No more Baudelaire. Smiling shyly, Rimbaud takes a virginally pink Emily by the hand, and now carries his burden a little more easily. And Verlaine staggers, miserable, nobody offered him any coffee, his genius is unappreciated. A proud Ezra Pound leaves the cafeteria. He is appreciated. In which hospital is Ezra Pound being treated? Nietzsche raises his arm in a Hitlerian gesture, shouts "I love you, Ariadne!" and leaves through a door opened by Ženia. And Garšva's mother swims out backward, her last gaze fading.

"Don't jump out the window, Stanley. It isn't necessary. Don't be a Thomas Wolfe character. Do you know how Thomas Wolfe died? Screaming. They sliced open his skull, but couldn't save him. Before the operation they cut off Wolfe's hair. His sister said it was beautiful, dark hair."

Stanley continued, as though he hadn't heard Garšva's words.

"Do you know what I'm waiting for? My youth holds me back. I live on Avenue B, on the fourth floor. The stairs are in bad shape. The rooms are dark. The toilet doesn't flush, you have to pull the handle several times. My mother mumbles something in Polish. My father sleeps, whether he's drunk or sober. Can you imagine how much fun it was on weekends? When I came home from my music lessons? How can you? I used to take that girl to some joint on the corner. For ice cream. A dark joint. Heavenly. I can still hear Mozart. *Dziękuję.* But one day I'll jump. To hell with heaven. And the bed. The clerk can have the bed."

"You won't jump, Stanley."

"You think?"

"You want to live, and that's why you're saying that you'll jump."

"You don't know America, Tony. We're doubles who have just met. I'm not going to weigh the 'for' and 'against', like you Europeans."

And Stanley glances at his watch.

"Time to go," he says. They get up and leave.

Can my youth save me? If I were to write a poem about it, I would probably say what others have already said. It would be a fragile, gentle nostalgia. Marshland. Spruce and birches. A fallen telegraph pole. An old horse dragging itself along a loamy road. A noble lie. Truth can't be pinned down. But... soon I'll crawl into the truth. And up *ir* down, up *ir* down. And here's the ninth.

Chapter 12

From Antanas Garšva's Notebooks

I was twenty-one, living in Kaunas, studying literature, making some extra money playing billiards.

Laisvės alėja was being modernised.[79] The round cobblestones and tracks for horse-drawn trolley buses disappeared. The street was paved with big-city asphalt. The now wealthy government erected elegant almost-skyscrapers. Red buses softly rocked bouncy-hipped ladies and pointy-whiskered, romantically inclined gentlemen with tailored shoulders as sharp as icebreakers. Artists just back from Paris tossed around French names at Konradas Café and spent hours drinking a single cup of coffee.[80] Bookstore windows displayed current art albums, magazines and books. The State Theatre experimented with lavish productions and announced famous touring performers every week. A

---

79 Laisvės alėja or Freedom Avenue: a 1700-metre pedestrian boulevard running through the centre of Kaunas, from the Old Town to the Church of Saint Michael the Archangel (popularly called the "Soboras", a variation on "Sobor," the Russian word for a Russian cathedral. The large, square neo-Byzantine church was built as a Russian Orthodox garrison church in 1895, when Kaunas was still part of the Russian Empire.). With two rows of linden trees, planters and benches, and many shops and restaurants, it was the social and business hub of the city during the interwar period, when it was also Lithuania's temporary capital while Vilnius was occupied by Poland.

80 Konradas Café: an interwar artists' cafe on Laisvės alėja.

jaded mulatto sashayed sexily at the Versalis Hotel and a well-known engineer overpaid for a night with her.[81] Dandies drank and boasted, wearing loud neckties for which they had also paid too much, as they had with the mulatto.

Asphalt ringed the mature linden trees. The most handsome policemen in the Baltics strode down the boulevard, white-coated hot-dog vendors smoked phlegmatically, and famous opera singers paraded by as though in a scene from *Othello*. Numerous beer halls opened, complete with slot machines and the clamour of second-rate artists, writers, functionaries.

And amid the sparkling of the bright lights, new houses, asphalt, linden trees, policemen, hot-dog vendors and dandies, a new Juozapota, a half-mad old woman, known as Madame Kukureku, no longer paid any attention to "how many gentlefolk, how handsome they are," but shuffled along, talking to herself.[82]

And when it got dark, and lanterns lit up the dark halos of the linden trees, groups of streetwalkers poured, like believers on a church feast day, on to the sidewalks, their teeth flashing the price of temptation. And high school students loitered on the sidewalks, greedily inspecting them. And the icebreaker-shouldered lovers, escorting their coiffured and fashionably Western mistresses or potential wives to American films, pretended not to notice them.

And a long-haired poet sauntered along the boulevard, his head thrown back as though he were trying to divine the mystery of the stars. The ends of his professional cravat waved rhythmically on his unwashed shirt front, and he had stuffed cardboard into his shoes because the soles had long since worn through. In his imagination sweep-poles rose and fell, cockerels announced the dawn, and the flowering

81 Versalis Hotel: a posh interwar hotel and restaurant on Laisvės alėja.

82 Juozapota: a character in *A Sad Story*, a novella by Jonas Biliūnas (1879–1907).

136

linden trees along Laisvės alėja were as fragrant as they'd have been at the edge of a field.

I was happy that evening. A few dozen litas jangled in my pocket.[83] I had found a victim from Panevėžys and really milked the little bald landowner – first losing, then cautiously and insecurely doing a bit better, then disastrously losing again, until, after a few successful rounds and admired by a lot of swearing bystanders, I stuffed the money into my pocket and left the bald landowner slurping his beer with trembling lips.[84]

I took a deep breath as I walked along Laisvės alėja. I had two or three days to myself, and I held my head high, savouring my success. My fingers had slithered along the green baize, my eyes measured the distances accurately, my cue had struck with precision, and impossible shots dropped into the pockets.

Suddenly I felt something new. A faint tremor rolled in waves down my spine. I felt dizzy. A strange thought crossed my mind – "Am I changing?" I paused by the cinema. "Is Laisvės alėja changing?" I leaned against the glass. The waves were still rolling down my back. "I must be tired from playing," I thought to myself, and then noticed Ženia. Small, clean, conscientious, a cheerful little tramp on a workday. I grabbed her by the arm and pulled her into the shadows of an alleyway.

"So you won today?" she asked probingly.

"I won," I replied.

"Do you want me?" Ženia asked further. I didn't reply.

"I think that first of all you need a drink," Ženia decided.

"You're right. Wait here. I'll run into the store. Tonight we'll drink red krupnikas.[85]

"I like you. And not just for the red krupnikas, as you know," said Ženia frankly.

---

83 Litas: the Lithuanian currency during the interwar period of independence

84 Panevėžys: the fifth largest city in Lithuania

85 Krupnikas: a spiced Lithuanian honey liqueur.

"You're unpretentious, and you don't swear when you're drunk. You'll be my first today. I'll make you happy, honey."

I fished in my pocket and pulled out a two-litas coin.

"Take it, in case I forget. I've owed you for two weeks. Thanks."

Ženia tossed the coin into her purse.

"No problem, honey. I'll always lend you some if you need it."

She spoke these words in a warm, familiar way, and I ran my fingers through her fluffy hair.

I was back on Laisvės alėja. The strange new feeling had passed. I went into a grocery store and purchased vodka, *krupnikas*, cigarettes, sprats, ham, butter, bread and chocolate.

I remember that night. The fragrant linden trees, my light steps, Ženia's hand which I clasped like a fiancée's, the slim museum tower, the sky, the moon, the stars, my neighbourhood Žaliakalnis, and the key with which I unlocked the door. I made love to Ženia, and that night I loved Ženia fleetingly. This contradiction didn't bother me. I had moved to another room and was lying to Jonė: I told her I was living with a respectable family and couldn't invite her over. We would make love in the countryside or my friend's room. I deceived Jonė because I was young, strong and confident. I was alive. I was sincerely happy. It wasn't the ecstasy I had experienced in Palanga – that had been diluted with a heavy dose of acting. This was youth. And tonight – in the company of the hustler Ženia.

I woke at ten the next morning. Ženia had left. She was good about leaving in time. A blend of odours hung in the room: alcohol, leftover food, exhaled breath. I stretched my limbs in bed. The slight pungency of copulation. I jumped up and opened the window. The sweet smell of the linden trees floated through the room and washed away the night. I grabbed a chair and pulled myself up. My wrists were shaking slightly. "Everything's fine," I thought to myself. I tidied up, shaved, bathed, put on a light grey suit and went out into the street.

I have trouble recalling the final steps. I once again sensed that the world was shifting. First I was overwhelmed by details: the dirty handle of the funicular car, the woman seated facing me, something in the corner of her mouth – a breadcrumb, here a single linden blossomed alone among thousands, a bus trundling along with a piece of newspaper stuck to one of its tires, and that man used black polish on yellow shoes. And it felt strange that I had locked my room, that the key was in my pocket, that I had got into and out of the funicular. And that those several minutes were no more than the sudden burst of a passing instant.

I was standing on Laisvės alėja by the window of the Maistas grocery store.

Zoori! Give me *zoori!* My wallet is full, I'm nicely dressed, shop girls smile at stylish young men like me. It's a beautiful day. I'll buy myself a book. I'll crack it open in the park and then continue to get to know it in my room. Today's lectures are in the afternoon, and I don't need to play pool tonight. I'll go to the cinema with Jonė. A few more steps to the bookstore. It's right there.

Zoori! Is this the world – is this what they call the Earth? This polished glass? These houses, trees, the Soboras, the policemen, the people, are they all real?[86]

I let out a muted cry. The short sound escaped and passers-by might have thought that a young man was belching after a big night. I clenched my fists, my teeth. I could feel my facial muscles twitching. I wanted to raise my arms and scream from the bottom of my lungs. To break back into the old world.

But I was leaning against the Maistas storefront. I could see my face in the glass. Its vague contours, greyish colour, mechanical twitching. Is this what it was like a million years ago? The sea murmurs, giant turtles crawl, my sharp nails

86   See note 104 re. "Soboras".

139

scratch at the damp sand. An awareness of what death will be like: death is only a door to an even more horrifying world. Where there is no more body, only nightmares created on Earth live there.

Zoori! Zoori, rescue me! I almost ran along Laisvės alėja, passing pedestrians, shoving them without apology. *Zoori, zoori*, the word penetrated me. Fine metal arrows whizzed in my ears. They chased me. Go, go. Details flew past me, important as in a dream. A girl's blue eyes, a stuffed briefcase. Both the eyes and the briefcase frightened me. As though I had seen ghosts I would be forced to live with forever.

The psychiatrist was the most famous one in Kaunas. I sat before him in a leather armchair. I was questioned, tapped, poked. I awaited his verdict. The psychiatrist's Jewish face exuded a mysterious foreignness. He twirled his pen and had yet to write out a prescription. This pause was filled with sounds from beyond the window: car horns, pedestrians shouting, a factory whistle travelling all the way from Aleksotas.[87] "The overture," I thought to myself. I shifted in the armchair.

"Do you still feel unwell?"

"Something keeps squeezing my throat, then releasing it."

"It will soon pass. The medication has not yet taken full effect."

The psychiatrist tapped his pen on the table.

"I imagine you would like to hear my diagnosis?"

"Yes."

"It is not as terrible as you imagine. We are no longer in Ibsen's times, and something you have inherited needn't destroy you. Of course, you will have to live moderately, I must emphasise that, but I do not believe that you will lose your mind or die. You are a neurasthenic."

"Will I recover?"

The pen rested quietly in his fingers.

---

87   A suburb of Kaunas on the left bank of the Nemunas, across from the city centre.

"It's difficult to say. I'm not a practitioner of rose-coloured diagnostics. But we'll try. What you've told me leads me to speak openly. Your disease is not yet fully understood. You know, the nervous system – these are labyrinths in which we are still quite lost."

He mumbled something in Latin that I didn't understand. Then he said, "You die and are risen again from the dead."

The psychiatrist grinned, probably pleased with his clever description of the disease.

"A passing nightmare," he added. And began to write out the prescription. The music from beyond the window continued to play. The now quiet whistle from the factory in Aleksotas still buzzed in my ears. Two men stopped outside the window.

"You're wrong – Banaitis is no good."

"I don't believe it. Yesterday he…"

The psychiatrist closed the window and I missed the rest of the conversation. I put two banknotes on the table.

"I want to get married," I blurted out.

"I would not advise it. You'll be a burden on your wife. If you need a woman…" and he grinned, like before.

"I understand, Professor. Thank you and goodbye."

"Come back in a month. Goodbye."

I went back out on to the street. I held the verdict in my hand. A white prescription. I studied the words. Some kind of bromide. The injection was working. I felt sleepily calm. Objects and people no longer frightened me. At the drugstore I received a red-capped bottle. I had lunch at the fancy Metropolis restaurant. And, when I returned home, I slept the kind of sleep that is free of dreams.

When I woke up it was evening. My date with Jonė was in half an hour. I felt oppressed by the scent of the linden trees, the lights starting to flicker on the slope of Aleksotas, the cool evening air, the muffled rattling on the streets, my stiff muscles, Jonė's kind eyes, those fateful words: "I will marry you."

I shouted out louder than I had earlier in the day by the Maistas store. I slammed the window shut. I took the bromide. I moaned into my clenched fists in the twilight. Until the sedative washed over me.

...Now she's walking, stopping by the post office, glancing at the arms of the clock. Two minutes past nine. He's a little late, she thinks to herself, finds a shoe store, takes a look at the latest style from Switzerland. Fifteen minutes past nine. Jonė walks slowly, every man is the one she is waiting for. Twenty minutes past nine. Maybe he's sick, she would go and visit him but doesn't know his address. Exactly half an hour. Jonė goes home...

It's over, Antanas Garšva. You'll sleep with Ženia or some other one, when you need a woman. You'll play much more pool. You'll sit in bars with talkative friends. You'll study literature more seriously. Of course, if you start thinking, "I can't live like this," you could kill yourself. But... you have a strong will to live, toned muscles, a healthy heart, clean lungs, good digestion. It's over, so start again, Antanas Garšva.

I was sentimental that evening. I felt sorry for myself. And I wrote Jonė a letter. I wanted to break up because I was bored to death with her.

A few weeks passed and I wrote a poem. It was my twentieth or so, and I timidly went to Konradas Café, where I hoped to meet a critic I knew. The critic was sitting by himself in a corner of the café, reading a French newspaper. We had met at Versalis and I had once asked him to take a look at my poems. When he gave them back to me I had detected an ironic sympathy in his expression. The critic was bent from consumption, wore spectacles, reddish shadows stretched across his grey face. That time he had said, "You want to be a poet?"

"I do," I replied.

"None of this is yours. You're searching for a 'classical' image, metre, rhyme. It's artificial, young man. You're different. I wouldn't recommend this rubbish to any serious magazine."

He noticed my disappointment.

"I'm not saying that you can't write. Try. But... don't depend merely on technique. Poetry is a demanding mistress. She despises con men and impotents. You're probably good at billiards, right?"

"Quite good," I boasted.

"That's what I thought after reading these," and the critic handed back the sheaf of papers.

Today I approached him quietly. I pulled up a chair, the critic stirred, the glass of his spectacles flashed, and he put his newspaper on the little table.

"Sit down."

I sat down, crumpling the single poem in my pocket. His glasses were searchlights pointing at the hand in my pocket.

"You've done some more writing?"

I pulled out the sheet of paper.

"Only one?" he said in feigned surprise. He took the sheet, carefully straightened it out, and started to read. He read much longer that I had expected, as the poem wasn't very long. And, when he had finished, he asked me in a warm, pleasant voice, "What is the matter with you? Are you ill?"

I felt my lips tremble, tears gather in my eyes.

"An incurable disease," I replied.

"It's not a bad poem," said the critic. "I'll try to get it published."

*

A tall brown man enters the empty elevator on the eighteenth. His face looks like it was carved from a pumpkin. A grown-up in a Halloween mask. Lips turned up at the corners, round, colourless eyes, an inflated forehead – like a genius, or someone with dropsy. A bald head, thick triangular eyebrows. A polka-dotted sports suit, the narrow jacket cinched at the waist. The brown man smiles evenly, his large, yellow, pointed teeth leaning against his upper lip.

"Down. Press 'pass'," the man orders colourlessly.

"Are you a … hotel employee?" asks Garšva.

"Yes."

Garšva presses the "pass" button, the elevator plunges down, no one can stop it at the intervening floors.

"Nice summer," notes the man.

"Very."

"*Felix culpa* doesn't suit you. I think you have already entered autumn."

"You can read my mind?" asks Garšva.

"A little. And I see a certain disproportion."

"In me?"

"Absolutely correct. The right side of your face is somewhat crooked. To be sure, the crookedness is barely noticeable, but in photographs…"

"I resisted slithering into this world. They pulled me out with forceps. The doctor pressed a bit too hard and… that's why I always have my picture taken at an angle," says Garšva, interrupting.

"That's what I wanted to emphasise."

The brown man's hands are thick and freckled.

"Are you … Irish?" asks Garšva.

"I'm not interested in my past, because I don't have one. But you – you're a different story. I'm not being critical, it's normal, you're following an ancient tradition."

"Excuse me, but…"

The man looks at Garšva. An experienced priest with a thorough knowledge of sinners.

"It's too late."

"Too late for what?"

"*O Felix culpa quae talem et tantum meruit habere redemptorem.*[88] You haven't forgotten?"

"I can't."

"There you are."

"If you remember," Garšva quickly begins to explain, "If

_____
88   See note 34.

you remember I kept thinking and thinking, when I was praying, that I want to make up for everything."

"It's too late," says the man, waving a freckled hand.

"You like to dream about Christ. Did Christ talk about his past?"

How long the elevator falls without stopping at any of the floors in between! And it occurs to Garšva that he would like to always have this person by his side, to always be able to talk to him.

"Then the devil took him to the holy city, to the top of the temple, and said: 'If you are the Son of God, jump down,'" says Garšva.

"Megalomania is not dangerous for you," the man says gently.

He glances at the numbers. They no longer light up, they are just dark ornaments at the edge of the ceiling. But the elevator continues to fall.

"Jonė's feet in their little white shoes," the man says colourlessly. "And your father staring at Pažaislis Monastery. And your mother screaming on a dying Earth. And two soft, sticky cherries, and a single poem on a crumpled piece of paper. And the smiling old woman."

"And *lioj, ridij, augo?*" Garšva asks hopefully.

"A *vėlė* wrapped in a white sheet. Your salvation."

"I'll pick up all the shards," Garšva promises. He would so like to touch the freckled hand, but doesn't dare.

"I won't forget you."

"You will. And now here's the lobby," says the man.

"The lobby already?"

"Yes, already. Do you remember the story about the angel and the newborn?"

"No."

"When an angel says goodbye to a newborn, he touches its face with a finger, so that the new arrival on Earth won't remember Heaven. That's why there is a little groove between the nose and the upper lip. Your face is slightly crooked in photographs. Do you see the connection?"

Garšva looks at the man's face. The Halloween mask is missing that groove.

"You don't have a groove – you don't have one!" exclaims Garšva.

"*Zoori*. The only word. It's a good word. Dream about *zoori*. It's good to dream about *zoori*. And now... open the door."

Chapter 13

"I trusted him. He's strong. He's successful. He bought a car, our savings are growing, he's looking at a house in Jamaica. I can't complain. He's caring and uncomplicated."

"And you're free to dream of Vilnius?"

"Don't make fun of me. You should know – I'm not afraid of work. I worked in a sewing factory for two years. I could start working tomorrow. You don't believe me?"

"Forgive me. Your husband. Try to understand."

"I do understand. I've been faithful to you these last two weeks."

"You…"

"We don't make love that often. But I think he'll want me again soon."

"And?"

"You decide."

"You would leave him?"

"Yes."

"I've saved up a bit. I'll buy another sofa. This one is too narrow to sleep on. Come, I'll be waiting."

"If I want to go back to the sewing factory, they'll take me. I was a good worker."

In his blue housecoat Garšva looked tired and wan. The wrinkles around his eyes deepened, the corners of his lips drooped, he touched his face with trembling fingers. He sat in the armchair, a sheaf of papers held together with a rubber band lay on the table.

"You read my notes?"

Elena lay on the sofa. A grey, little woman under a blue-covered quilt.

147

"I found it painful. Don't be angry – I'm not talking about the literary quality."

She stopped talking.

"Grotesque?" asked Garšva.

"You're anxious, so it's grotesque."

"And your noblemen's heads?" interrupted Garšva bitingly.

"That's why we met."

"Two grotesques."

"We need to be together. That's not grotesque."

"You're not afraid of this..." asked Garšva, looking at the pack of papers.

"We need to be together. And I'll help you."

Garšva grabbed the bottle of White Horse.

"Don't drink," Elena asked.

"I'm afraid of death, so I drink. I'm afraid of death, so I write. I'm afraid of death, so I take pills. Everything is because of death. The poet Vaidilionis said that trees covered in toadstools are ironic. My life is ironic. Let's say, for example, that an optimistic writer is sitting in his study. I imagine that his feet are pedicured, there's a subtle scent of cologne, a pleasant atmosphere. You reach out your arm. An ivory paperweight. You reach out your arm. Chagall's illustrations for *Dead Souls*. You reach out your arm. Plato and a Platonic god. And if it's too dull, there's a Renoir hanging on the wall. It's heaven on earth. And so interesting how the Negro mask is used! And the lawn in the park is trimmed – perfection, harmony. My own atmosphere, I'm afraid, is nothing but passed gas, a cosy stench. I would be a grotesque if I tried to be a Plato. Maybe, if I got myself a job as a night watchman, I might be able to squeeze out some Faustian stories for little children. Isn't suffering – no matter how lovely – grotesque? Van Gogh shot himself in a field, and his blossoming cherries are so lovely! Poe drank himself to death, and the cries of his raven are so lovely! Čiurlionis ran from the madhouse through the snow, and his sonata paintings are so exquisitely musical![89] 'Kill me, doctor, or you're a murderer,' begged Kafka. This Jew is indeed charming with his horrifying nightmares!"

"I'm sorry, you're angry, and that…"

"I know, I'm contradicting myself. And I'm jealous. And illogical. You're right. I mock. I admire. I drink, I love. Because I like to drink, love and mock. If I find a harmonious truth, I'll have lost. And I'll lose if I fail to find truth."

Two red circles appeared on Garšva's cheeks. He drank half a glass in one gulp. His whitened fingers squeezed the glass tight. Elena shifted. Garšva placed the glass on the table.

"You rest. I feel better when you're lying here. Stay."

"Don't drink," she repeated.

"Stay."

It was damp outside. Cool. Thirty-eight white bathrobes hung on a line, Garšva counted them as he waited for Elena. The shutters of the adjacent house were closed, and rippling flames from the chimney of a distant foundry burst through the clouds.

"My jeweller is lazy. He didn't tighten the carnelian ring. You and I didn't visit the wagon in the square in Plaza. We're émigrés, we need anachronisms. You need legends, I – unfinished poems."

"What does your doctor say?"

"Nothing definitive."

"When will you see him?"

"Tomorrow."

Garšva suddenly moved to the sofa. He leaned his hands against Elena's shoulders.

"You want to live with me? It would be good. I'll stop drinking, I'll smoke less. I'll change my shift so we can be together in the evenings. Once in a while I'll ask you to go

---

89 Čiurlionis: the early modernist Lithuanian painter and composer Mikalojus Konstantinas Čiurlionis (1875–1911).

out – to a movie or visit friends. I'll write. I won't mock you any more. It'll be good for me to be with you. I would like to say a few words. Final words. For myself. I'd like to write a cycle of poems in which each letter is an irreplaceable ornament. I would work long and hard to find them. I feel good with you. Don't think that I'm talking like this because I'm drunk. This is my obsession. A few lines etched into marble, that's what I long for. The illusion of immortality? So be it. To die with a real illusion is the real thing. I will give thanks. To my father, my mother, the marshland, the semaphore, Jonė, my seizures, my critic, books, the soaking old woman, Ženia, Vaidilionis. All of them. If you think we can try, then let's try. I may win. If you believe in me, then stay. If you need me too."

"I love you," said Elena. "I'll speak to my husband today. And I'll be here."

"You don't need to. I'll ask him for the divorce myself."

Time dissolved. Clenched fingers, final sacrifice, the sliding downwards, the reward of an animal cry.

And oblivion for one of the winners. For Antanas Garšva. His muscles loosened. All that was left in his dimming consciousness was the silhouette of a right arm. And he didn't even feel himself slip off the sofa. He managed to grab his blue robe, his fingers clutching a silk edge.

Antanas Garšva lay on the flowered linoleum. His mouth was ajar, and a green foam leaked from it, ran down his cheek and dripped on to a spectacular flower. His pupils disappeared into his eyelids. His legs were curled under him, like a sleeping child's. His fingers and toes were turning yellow. Elena grabbed and threw on her dress, ran to the kitchen and came back with a bowl of water. She tilted the bowl towards Garšva's head.

A broad stream splashed on to his nose and ran down his face to the floor. His consciousness and pupils gradually returned. The skin below one nipple quivered, the heart was beating. His fingers released the edge of his robe. With

Elena's help, Antanas Garšva got back on to the sofa. He wiped his wet face with one hand. Sweat poured out his pores, his body glistened like an oiled athlete's.

"Shoes," he said. "Van Gogh's shoes. I saw them. It made me angry. Dirty shoes on a table. Give me a cigarette."

"Wait a bit. Drink some water."

Elena scooped up some water from the bowl, and Garšva took the glass.

"There's a little box in my trouser pocket. Give it to me."

He carefully opened the lid of the box and shook two celluloid bullets on to his palm, tossed them into his mouth and drank some water. Then he slipped on his robe and tied it at the waist. He took out a handkerchief and wiped his face.

"How did I look when I was unconscious?"

"Don't ask, it isn't necessary."

"How did I look when I was unconscious?"

"You were lying on the linoleum, your legs curled, clutching your robe."

"That'll have to do. Like a Venetian doge who poisoned himself by his lover's bed. Or like a slain beast in a pool of blue blood. That's how a romantic would resolve it. Leave me now. I'll go to sleep."

"What is your doctor's phone number?"

"There's no need to call him. It's not the first time. When one of these attacks is over, I don't need a doctor any more. I'll sleep and I'll be fine again."

"You don't want me to stay?"

"No. It's a strange psychological reaction. I want to be alone. It helps. I'll explain it all to you later. Forgive me."

"I'll come tomorrow. I'll come with my things."

"No, not tomorrow. I'll call you. I might be at the doctor's. I'll call you tomorrow."

Elena put her coat on in silence and Garšva lit a cigarette. He got up without difficulty and kissed Elena, his lips warm with life.

"Be sure to call me tomorrow."

"I will. Thank you, forgive me."

"I love you," said Elena. And she left.

Garšva poured some White Horse into his glass. He drank it. He glanced through the window. The thirty-eight bathrobes still hung there, the shutters were still closed, the glimmers of sunlight were still trying to break through the clouds.

"That was the first time. The first time that I fainted. What does it mean?"

"What!" he shouted. A warm sensation of calm slowly blanketed his brain.

"Why didn't I tell her that I've spent time in a mental hospital? Why didn't I write about it?"

*

It begins to get crowded at around ten o'clock. The young people's dance on the eighteenth – young men and women from the curtain factory in Brooklyn will be whooping it up. The Masonic dinner finished a while ago. On time. Rosy old men and ladies in multicoloured paper hats – their Medieval heritage – travelled downward, bells tinkling atop their respectable heads. They blew into small cardboard tubes, making obscene red blobs poke out. Some of the men tried to drop lifelike rubber frogs or lizards into their ladies' décolletés. And chuckled.

Now the young people are going up. They go up looking sad, holding on to each other. The colours of the paper hats are reincarnated in the girls' dresses, earrings, fake flowers, their cheeks and eyebrows; in the young men's ties, buckles, socks.

They go up in pairs, barely speaking, looking into each other's eyes. They've been condemned to dance. They stare into each other's eyes as though they were splitting up. An upside-down world. The people going down are having fun. This is a dolls' party held in a funeral parlour.

Some are already drunk as they go up. They smoke cheap

cigars and try to make conversation with the same words they use in the factory. Nylon curtains collect a lot of static, so when you hang them on the metal rods you can get shocks in your fingers. These yellow flowery curtains make you cough when you cut them, because of all the starch floating in the air. And it's really fun with the plain white curtains, the scissors slice them real fast – and the day's work flies by. Garšva learns all of this from the ones going up without girls.

"Right, Mac, it's tough for you too."

"I guess I have a good stomach."

"Right, Mac, tomorrow it'll be more curtains."

"Too bad we just got the hall from ten o'clock."

"Yes, the factory is celebrating its anniversary. We don't pay, the bosses pay."

"The new foreman is too picky. All the new ones are picky."

How beautifully the curtains fluttered in Cocteau's film! The long castle hallway, the open windows, the wind, and the white curtains. The same ones that make the day go quickly when you're cutting them.

The young people from the curtain factory. A dolls' party. The curtains – a symbol of insolubility. Someone stirred on the other side, and Polonius fell, having been stabbed. Curtains – a symbol of solubility. Othello grabbed the curtains one last time. I like curtains. They're alive, like dolls. They're eternal in their softness, just as dolls are in their fixed expressions. A subtle combination: dolls hanging from curtains. Let them flutter in the wind. Sad embracing couples. Two hearts pierced by one arrow. A Cupid with good aim walks through a green field, his legs are pink and his nails pearly.

"Right, Mac. Want a cigar? Here."

An upside-down world. Why aren't you Masons, and the Masons – you? A gangly young man, still pink from Cupid's arrow, kisses his girlfriend's neck. They're pressed against the wall. The doll watches the numbers, mouth ajar, and Garšva waits for someone to squeeze her and for the girl to say "Ma-ma".

Your floor. The eighteenth, eighteen-year-olds. Kiss while you dance; kiss on the velvet sofas, the ones in the hotel corridors, I won't see it. And forget about the curtains. *Ave Caesar, vivantes te salutant!*[90]

Strange. The sad couples have brought me hope. Every day, every hour enriches me. I chose a great job. I can even imagine that I picked it on purpose. I no longer have to trudge through the rain. The old woman, a dutiful camp resident, did her bit and lies blessed and rotting in her grave. And the poet Vaidilionis writes poems about a real *vaidila* he borrowed from the Romantics – one who never played nineteenth-century melodies on the *kanklės* at the times of the crusades.[91] And he stuffs his stanzas with Jericho flutes. So that the wind orchestra, in which only the cornet comes close to actually playing, can play a funeral march.

---

90 *Ave Caesar, vivantes te salutant*: "Hail Caesar, the living salute you, which is a play on "Ave Caesar, morituri te salutant", which means, "Hail Caesar, those who are about to die salute you."

91 *Vaidila*: a high priest in the Lithuanian pre-Christian religion; "Vadilionis" is an ironic play on this word. *Kanklės*: a Lithuanian string instrument of the zither family.

Chapter 14

From Antanas Garšva's Notebooks

The smallish DP camp had been planted on a bare Bavarian field.[92] Four barracks nailed together by Russian prisoners of war. On the loamy ground. As we walked through the rain to pick up our food rations, clumps of earth stuck to our canvas shoes, impossible to wash off. Clothing was distributed to us – leftover Canadian forest-ranger uniforms. We ripped off the badges and guarded a few ratty shrubs, our anxiety, our hungry anger, our grotesque rations (which for some reason included an excess of toilet paper), our dark green hopes.

And we elected committees. And celebrated our national holidays. And excited speakers shouted: "We will return next year!" And we wept when a six-year-old girl recited a poem that repeatedly mentioned our country's name. And in the evenings men sat by the barracks belting out songs, the verses repeating rhythmically until the last note faded.

92   Displaced persons (DP) camp. At the end of the Second World War, refugees from Lithuania and other Eastern European countries, and survivors of Nazi concentration camps, were housed in DP camps located in Allied-controlled Germany, Austria and Italy. Here they awaited visas to the countries accepting post-war refugees/immigrants, primarily the United States, Canada and Australia. The Lithuanian DP community included members of the intelligentsia, business and government leaders, who quickly established their own social, cultural and political organisations, as well as publications, sports teams and schools.

And I thought I saw a bright streak left by a shooting star, a freshly burnt meteor.

We were sentimental, exhausted, jealous, angry. And sexual. We seduced each other's wives, we made love in ditches dug by the *Volkssturm*, and forgot the previous night's embraces – often rushed, cowardly, unsuccessful – by morning. And some, who had managed to shed the past, traded in apples, jewellery, gasoline, cows – as if they were the reincarnated *vėlės* of incinerated tradesmen.

Four barracks, dropped on to the loamy earth. Mounds of scrap metal (airplane hangars, now destroyed by bombs, had once stood there) were our children's playground. The squelching of our canvas shoes in the mud – it rained often that year – and the interminable talk, in which a future chronicler would hear only one significant phrase: "When I lived in Lithuania…"

Two hundred people. Eighty-four men, eighty-two women, thirty-six children.

I had not written any poems for a long time, but I was up to date with the latest books and magazines, and wrote about Lithuanian and German theatre, painting exhibitions, concerts and books. That was how I scraped together the few marks I needed to buy alcohol.

My skills improved, and the agonies of hell began to look like Gulliver's adventures among the giants.

Providence had made me an observer of corpses. I saw many, and in different states. In East Prussia I saw a dead woman, she was lying next to a pear tree in full pink bloom. In Weimar I saw a group of uniformed schoolgirls pulled from a cellar, welded together by hot water during the bombing. Inflated, their faces the colour of those women who spend too much time under quartz lamps. By the Czechoslovak border we came across an abandoned, reeking freight wagon. When we opened it we found about thirty decomposing children, aged three to seven. We never learnt who had forgotten them on the reserve tracks.

Adult male corpses had no effect on me, as though I were an experienced gravedigger.

I was privileged and shared a small room with the poet Vaidilionis. I loathed his ascetic face, his deep-set eyes, his short, thickset body, his large hands (hundreds of his ancestors had scratched at the infertile earth, and his fingers were bent at the joints, like in a death agony), his coarse black hair combed on to his wide forehead in a special style, his yellow toenails which he liked to cut with a kitchen knife, his sacrilegious posture – the way he sat at the table writing poems, stiff and bobbing like a priest performing the elevation.

I followed Vaidilionis's rise. The Lithuanian newspapers and magazines published his poems on their front pages and his stern face with its meaningfully closed lips often gazed at the reader. Vaidilionis was recited by actors, amateurs and children; he was quoted by priests, camp officials and reviewers.

Vaidilionis versified effortlessly. He sprinkled our dark green hope with rosy hyssop. He didn't inscribe quiet melodies in the sand, he didn't scorch us with the slow fire of loss, he didn't wander amongst childhood's happy ghosts, and didn't look for a castle with clear windows, lanterns or gold carriages. Vaidilionis had a calming, uplifting effect. In a few tight stanzas the horrors of war would slink past and then a powerful voice (God's, some saint's or his own) would quickly scatter marble pedestals about the loamy earth and then place us on top of them. There we were in our narrow trousers, grey faces, just like the grand dukes of the past, heads full of fantasies like a poor servant girl. And on the highest pedestal stood Vaidilionis himself. A prophet on a block of stone.

And around all of this Vaidilionis masterfully arranged a thoughtful collection of props: a zinc-coloured Nemunas, varnished country beams, a father's talismanic pipe, a sprig of chamomile pressed in a prayer book, the star-studded wings of friendly angels, a patriotically howling dog.

And in the final stanzas the grand dukes popped up once again, calling us to a bright future. We, their natural successors, as brave as the legendary Vikings. We who scrabbled for every donated rag, we who waited for overseas passages and imagined ourselves enjoying sofas with firm springs, real, nicotine-rich cigarettes, creams, furs and fresh meat.

My very first meeting with Vaidilionis was disastrous. When I entered the room and threw my thin knapsack on to the floor, Vaidilionis was sitting on his cot, writing.

"Good day, aesthete Garšva," he said, setting aside his carefully penned manuscript sheets. We had known each other in Lithuania.

"Good day, Vaidilionis, you old corpse," I replied. He glanced at my shoes, which could not have been more pathetically worn out. I sat down on a stool.

"These shoes are a half-size too small. That's why my feet reek. Open the window, because the room will start to smell," I stated.

Vaidilionis looked at my shoes in silence, and I felt a mix of shame and irritation.

"Hide your poems. Temporarily. While I air out and wash my feet," I said, focusing on the frayed strings masquerading as laces.

"I feel sorry for you," said Vaidilionis, emphasising each consonant.

"And I for you."

Vaidilionis continued, as though he hadn't heard me.

"A number of years ago you and I had it out. You argued your position with paradoxes and supposedly won. You dismissed morality, idealism and the good Lord. You worshipped only literature. Now, I would dare to clarify, it was your own bile. I remember your illness. How many poems have you written in exile?"

"Since I escaped, none," I said.

I untied the strings and took off my shoes. And looked

glumly at the dirty toes peering quizzically through the remains of my socks.

"How many articles and reviews have you written?"

"Many."

"The washroom is at the end of the corridor," said Vaidilionis. "When you come back, we'll have a bite."

I took my time washing. I couldn't stand heavy streams of water. They stroked my skin like the caresses of a woman one has gotten sick of, on whom one has become sexually dependent.

When I returned I found Vaidilionis had arranged some preserves, bread and a bottle of beetroot vodka on the stool.

"So where have you been wandering? You lived somewhere privately after the war? I heard something from the editors," he said.

"I was lucky. I spent three months digging trenches in East Prussia. Then near Czechoslovakia. And escaped. I was only in one bombing in Weimar. And found a place to live in a village. A German lady took me in. I slept with her. I fertilised her garden with my family's manure. After a while she kicked me out."

"What for?"

"I drank too much."

"Are you going to try for America?"

"I'll try."

Vaidilionis followed my shaking hands as I sipped the beet spirits.

"Your hands tremble."

"I'm not dead yet. Unlike you."

"Explain," he said calmly.

"Some young guys got together in one of the camps," I started, greedily swallowing some canned beef. "They write poems. They read Eliot, Pound, others. They know Heidegger, Jaspers, Sartre. They love the new painting."

"They're untalented Western epigones," interrupted Vaidilionis.

"They believe in poetry. It's in their poems that I discovered a love for my country. A love for my childhood. For broken toys. And the question 'Why?' And the will to survive. Come to think of it, there's a colleague of yours in that other camp. He writes 'classical' poems, just like you. Old Homer is happily rubbing his hands in Hades. The little old Moirai watch him adoringly. But even they aren't interested in you."

"Be more specific."

"Your fate has been spun. You shout out big words about the past, bright words about the future. You're virtuous, or pretend to be. So you're lying."

"The alcohol is affecting you," said Vaidilionis in a cold, quiet voice, and drank some beet spirits. "Eat," he added.

Then he got up and stuck his hands in his pockets. He stood, and I contemplated the buttons on his jacket. "Fanatics and their followers tighten both their muscles and their souls," I thought to myself.

"And what are you, exactly?" he asked me.

"I'm waiting," I said, working on the last bits of meat.

"I know what you've gone through. I'll say it again. I feel sorry for you. But the end result is sad. You can't write any more. Envy makes the powerless angry. But at least you're honest. When you can't write, you don't. I respect you for that."

I did my best to keep my hands from trembling. I put some meat on a little piece of bread, lifted it slowly towards my mouth, and slowly sipped the spirits, holding the empty glass before my face.

"May I take a look at your latest poems?"

"You may. Read them, and, if you like, discredit them. But take note. I am published, read, recited. And they say – I sustain their will to live, their hope. The whole nation's hope."

And Vaidilionis passed me the sheets of manuscript. I read, and the blood in my head pulsed. Vaidilionis was still standing, his hands in his pockets.

I finished and placed the sheaf on the green blanket.

"A typical example of impotence. The word 'Lithuania' is squeezed in three times over four poems. The main idea in these poems is the racial nobility of the Lithuanian people. The technique is clean. You could advertise shoe polish. The images aren't demanding. Of course the air is cleaner in the woods. What was it that inspired Vytautas the Great on that green field? You yourself, in your green trousers?"

"My diagnosis is correct," Vaidilionis said quietly, shaking his head.

"Go ahead, shake your head, Mister Popular Poet! You'll be forgotten!"

"You've already been forgotten," Vaidilionis said calmly.

I said nothing. For four months.

In late fall, as the rain poured relentlessly down on the camp, an old woman died. The first of our barracks community to depart for the afterlife. There was nothing remarkable about the old woman. She had attended mass zealously, enjoyed the food rations, and died from a heart attack, though she had complained mainly of rheumatism in her legs. Since she was the first victim, it was decided that she should have a grand funeral.

By a strange coincidence, a former wind orchestra member lived in the camp. He was able to put together a band, because the UNRRA director, a fervently inebriated Ohio butcher, donated some instruments he had confiscated from the Germans.[93] The wind veteran rounded up a few young men and quickly taught them to play a march, "Two Clergymen Brothers," as well as a "Potpourri of Lithuanian Melodies", which some Jew had assembled in pre-war Lithuania. And for "dessert", as it was put by the bandleader who played the cornet and still wore a traditional moustache, the old woman's funeral would be celebrated with Chopin's *Marche funèbre*.

---

93 UNRRA: United Nations Relief and Rehabilitation Administration.

The old woman was clothed in a black dress which some merciful ladies had sewn from multicoloured rags and tinted with ersatz dye, so that the deceased's garment was embellished with green spots. The carpenter Rimšinis nailed together a coffin from the less rotten boards lying by an unfinished barracks hut. The bigger camp sent a priest, a pleasant man who smiled demurely if he heard a common swear word.

We had to walk a couple of kilometres to a tiny village with a grandiose name. To Koenigshafen. It was midday and the rain had stopped. We formed a procession. The Boy Scout Povilėnas carried the cross. The muffled-up priest trudged along in borrowed galoshes. The old woman bounced on a simple Swabian cart pulled by a thin horse with a strangely fat belly. And the brass band marched, proud and shining.

The old woman did not have any relatives, so the first rows were graced by the little camp's officials and a distinguished personage who gave speeches remarkable in their impressive use of ellipses.

We walked in harmonious silence for about a kilometre. The brass band procrastinated. The bandleader did not have much faith in his colleagues, he said he had only once been pleasantly surprised by their playing. Then it began to rain again. The rain sprayed horizontally into our faces and the horse's ears, drenched the Crucified One, the Boy Scout Povilėnas's hair, and fell on the coffin, forming brief puddles before streaming down its sides. The coffin was full of cracks and wider along the base, so the rain inevitably soaked the old woman's dress.

"The old woman is getting wet," I said to Vaidilionis, who was marching with meaningfully closed lips.

"Don't mock me," said Vaidilionis through his teeth.

"That's not what I'm doing. Cold skin and cold water. An unpleasant pairing. Why isn't the orchestra from Jericho playing?"

The bandleader waved his hand, and the musicians

pulled out green handkerchiefs and wiped off their dewy trumpets. The priest's galoshes squeaked like old taps. The road was still loamy and it seemed to me that I could feel the earth's sucking pull. The spire of the village church gradually appeared through the curtain of rain. We were surrounded by submerged fields, a cramped little world we longed to escape.

"Now the rain is melting the ersatz dye. The black liquid is dying the innocent old woman's skin. Quite an interesting effect. Black is the colour of funerals, after all, and Heaven tolerates human symbolism. If it rains any harder we'll end up burying a black woman."

Vaidilionis grabbed me by the shoulder. His wet face was ridiculous with rage. I squealed. Vaidilionis frothed.

"You're a paranoiac. You belong in a madhouse."

"Wipe your nose," I replied.

Suddenly the band piped up. We had approached the village vegetable plots, their summer huts lined up on the wet, naked earth. Chopin sounded in all his horror. The rookies blew into their trumpets, hitting neither the beats of the drum nor matching the bandleader's menacing upper body gestures. The sound of his cornet carved into an area of a few metres before the melody's harsh strokes dissolved.

"This old skeleton has almost filled his clarinet with spit," I said under my breath.

Vaidilionis broke away from me. Chopin collapsed. His patent leather shoes got scuffed, his shirt got wrinkled, he lost a lace cuff, got clay all over his stylish face, gravel tangled in his curls, and he let out a wail. He got chilled. Consumption? No, consumption is slow, Chopin caught a deadly case of pneumonia.

"Every generation experiences the end of the world," I said to the distinguished speech-maker.

"Look at the bandleader's moustache. It's wilting."

"What are you saying, sir?" asked the personage.

"The *Marche funèbre* is suitable for Laisvės alėja. For

burying a great state figure. A boy scout's drum would have been enough for a drenched old woman."

I turned around and returned to the camp. It rained until evening. As I learned later, the funeral procession found shelter in the village pub. I was alone for a few hours.

I wrote long lines. A complicated cocktail flowed through the trenches of my brain. I sat on my cot in my underpants, because my clothes were drying in the laundry room. As I produced stanza after stanza, I saw my marauding letters, my yellow, Swabian-tobacco-stained fingers, the photograph of Maironis above Vaidilionis's bed. I erected a totem in my mind: an unknown soldier and a soaked old woman, severe statues, kept my words in check.

Somewhere there was much light and transparent air. From the past, another town, another Kaunas came back to me. I spent a lot of time looking for a door hidden in a stucco wall. There were many small bumps on it. Too many. Yes, I was conscientious and spent a lot of time feeling the wall, looking for a button to press. But I didn't find it and lost strength. I stood paralysed by the invisible door and all I could do was describe the monotonous bumps, the abstract, repetitive relief.

A dutiful camp resident, a naive old woman who liked prayers and order in her little world, had passed away. And she was laid out, stuffed into a coffin in a dyed dress, and transported in the rain, angry and wet. In the greyness of the Swabian fields, in the grotesque funeral procession, I was allowed to stop and look back. A harmless old woman pressed a little bump that only she knew, and the door opened. Expecting no gratitude, my totem stretched out an arm to show me the way, and I entered obediently, my marauding letters accompanying me.

I worked for a week. Vaidilionis didn't bother me. We exchanged only essential phrases. Sometimes I felt his inquisitive gaze on my crown, my temples, my forehead. Nevertheless, Vaidilionis was tactful. I often jumped up and tried to walk around that wooden cage. Then Vaidilionis would leave, and I would be alone for two or three hours.

A week crept by, and the two of us were silently eating pea soup from tin cans. A sheaf of handwritten pages lay under my pillow.

"Salty soup," Vaidilionis said unexpectedly. His coiffured hair fell on his forehead in a so-called "unruly mop" which he curled every morning with a wide-toothed comb. In his agrarian hands the aluminium teaspoon was a titan's parody of a toy civilisation. An ascetic's face? Today I saw a combination of will, popular adulation and constipation.

"Peas aren't a good idea. They cause gas," I replied.

"We'll open the window. You're not writing any more today?" Vaidilionis's expression was pure. He used this expression on the stage, when reading his lyric poems.

"Your eyes are innocent today. Like that old woman's, the one we buried."

"You didn't bury her."

"That's correct. I immortalised her. In myself." I got up mechanically, pulled out the sheaf of papers and handed them to Vaidilionis.

"Read it. It's a first draft."

He read, and I observed his face. He pressed his lips together in stereotypical intensity. His coarse, straight eyelashes descended like jail bars. He must have already come across my hopeless trudging along the loamy road, the screeching of the trumpets, the muddy Chopin, the rain, and the peaceful, blackened old woman. And far away in the North, a series of Kaunas buildings walked by. The Soboras's elephantine feet trampled the little houses of Šančiai as they scattered to the sides. The red-brick cathedral snorted like a locomotive. A lone island poked out near Pažaislis Monastery. My mother was standing on it. She held a dirty piece of cloth embroidered with little crosses in her hands as angels and archangels hovered over her. An army of angels above a lost Kaunas. At night the angels poured sparkles over the city, their glowing hands slipped into the lanterns on Laisvės alėja, their wings cast long shadows on the icy pavement. And the mute brass band marched on. Their trumpets polished by the moonlight shone, the band was led by the devil, who had sewn a black-dyed rope to his velvet trousers. And the band was followed by a swaying coffin carried by four lighthouse keepers, and the old woman in the coffin sat up and smiled. A full moon floated by, as did my mother, Chopin's lace, the green Nemunas, the smiling old woman.

Vaidilionis was done. Not a single facial muscle quivered. His upper lip was still missing. He gave me back the sheaf of papers. I stuffed it under my blanket. I grabbed the empty cans.

"I'm going to go wash them," I said.

Vaidilionis glanced at me. The jail bars rose.

"What are you planning to call – that?"

"What do you mean – that?"

"That question. If you like, the whole poem is only a question."

I didn't answer, just clanged the empty cans. Like the cymbals in the band my poem had conjured up.

"This is bad news. Much worse than in Kaunas, when you still controlled yourself. I wouldn't want to argue that the lack of metre necessarily means a poet's decline. But you juggle with imagery ... in a meaningless manner. It's a cleverness inspired by neurasthenia. You can dismiss my opinion, but this isn't the time to be thinking about ourselves. We have to think about the nation. I don't expect you to imitate anyone. Write about yourself. But remember – intellectual neurasthenia and decadence are one and the same thing."

"You speak clearly. Periods, commas. It's a pity I don't do shorthand. If I did, I would have your words put up on a bulletin board," I said, no longer clanging the cans.

"You're trying to be ironic. Irony is part of your pathology.

You saw trees covered with toadstools, which are ironic. But are they healthy?"

And Vaidilionis carefully stroked his special hairstyle. My arms hung down, and the cans hung down from my fingers like weights from a scale.

"We'll find ourselves a judge." I swung a can in the direction of Maironis's photograph.

"Maybe him? Though I fear he would condemn you ... for being an actor who recites for actors. You should be reciting your poems in Lithuania, in the forest.[94] Those men and women awaiting their deaths would listen to you. Your patriotism would be one more weapon for them. Here you are safe and receive a salary. It's obscene."

A spark flashed across Vaidilionis's pure expression. He stood up.

"But still, I respect you. For your technique. 'And the homeland will be free!' Change a few letters. 'And the homeland we won't flee.' Your technique is unrivalled. You know, you remind me of another poet. Zuika. Remember him? You're both cynics. But, pardon me. You're stupider. Soon you'll be convinced you're some kind of missionary."

"Get out of the room! Get out this minute!" Vaidilionis shrieked. I launched the left can at the window. It broke the grimy glass and landed at the feet of an ex-general's wife who happened to be walking by.

"The *poe*-ets are *fie*-ting!" shouted the ex-general's wife in the yard.

Vaidilionis ran out the door. I broke out in convulsive, hysterical laughter.

There was the bed, covered with the green blanket, depressions showing where I had sat. And higher up, on the wall, hung Maironis. I walked to the washroom, waving a can. The hallway had filled with camp residents.

The doctors examined me thoroughly but found no signs of insanity. I was moved to another camp.

94   See note 61 re. "Forest Brothers".

*

Antanas Garšva is smiling. Strange that these are the kinds of things that I recorded. I left out equally important ones. I killed a man, I wanted to kill myself, I was beaten, I survived, unconscious, in Aukštoji Panemunė, in a Kaunas hospital. All that has faded. But there are things I should remember. Those who walked beside me. I bathed my surroundings in the green of an El Greco Toledo landscape. I shortened the perspective. My Valley of Josaphat is the size of a room. My childhood, my youth are the size of a room. I was too negative about my past. I chose the same method as those who extract only elegiac sadness from theirs. I had fewer crystals, of course. But they still sparkled. I emphasised a *particular attitude* towards my own reality. And I was given more hours in which to find myself. Perhaps *they* were important, perhaps *they* are what I should focus on. Then I might be able to remember all that I missed. The Toledo landscape has bathed my unconscious. The crystals have been tossed into its darkest corner. I need to drag them back like keys stuck behind a cupboard. I have to stretch out on the floor, focus my entire being, and reach out my arm. Once I have the keys I'll be able to unlock the cupboard. Now I was looking at the cupboard's impenetrability, as though at mysterious curtains. I'll take a look inside the cupboard and then, may all the gods help me, I will understand the curtains.

"Oh yeah, it's not so bad. You get a few dozen dollars. Sometimes there's overtime. Do you do overtime? Want a cigarette?"

"Thanks. I'll smoke it later. It's not allowed in the elevator."

"Stupid box."

"Pretty stupid."

Garšva puts the cigarette in his breast pocket. I want to be happy, I want to live. Up *ir* down, forty dollars, happiness. There are counterarguments. It could be worse.

Cancer, labour camps, torture, losing loved ones. What's a breakup in comparison? I split up with Jonė, but I remember her when I feel sad. Sadness only lasts so long. It's a self-defence mechanism. A confession after which, for a while, it's a little more pleasant to live. My memory of Elena will fade away sadly like that. I'll write. And I should be happy. I'm alive and free. An absurd man, in Camus's terms? So be it. An absurd man who speaks to Christ. And with philosophers. That's okay. Philosophy is also an art. Fine. I'll see reality as material from which my soul will create eternity. Which will die with me, and which another newborn will glance at briefly before creating his own eternity. It doesn't matter that I won't have anyone to love. Hello, Professor Spinoza! There's a rumour that you threw yourself into philosophy after you were dumped by a girl?

Fine. My eyes are binoculars through which everything appears backwards. The world recedes as it comes into focus. I can make a stone sing about spring. I can order tulips to play a Gregorian resurrection. And what if Saint Anthony stands on the roof of a skyscraper in the moonlight, crossing himself because two shabby and obsequiously smiling *kaukai* have brought him a Lithuanian Ophelia. "Saint Anthony, you should give us some new pants – you're a saint after all." And my childhood friends could gather in Stevens's tavern: a girl who made me urinate in a wooden cup when we were pretending to be guests drinking tea, a kid with whom I used to bang telegraph poles, and then all my lovers, escorted by the three senior wives of the harem: Jonė, Ženia, Elena.

And Christ. We'll greet Him reverently. We'll kneel and kiss the edge of His garment. And Stevens will serve everyone the most expensive scotch, knowing that the bottle will always remain full. And we'll sing a hymn about childhood, life and death. And Christ will challenge His rival, Buddha. "Very well," Buddha will say. "I am a free, educated spirit. You are the Son of God. And I'll drink with

You, even if this means I'll be haunted by nightmares in nirvana. And Christ will touch Buddha's forehead with the palm of His hand and say: "No, they will not haunt you. You will rest in peace, Buddha." And Christ will serve Buddha, who had spoken earlier than He had.

Fine. My entire universe fits within me. Past, present, future. But I am not a superman. I am a manikin, swaddled in a dirty cotton apron, who wants to devote himself to self-revelation. I will ignore apparent reality. I won't be afraid of *auto-da-fé*. Let them lead me, barefoot, covered in a yellow mantle with a diagonal cross, let them hang long scapulars around my neck and press a yellow candle into my hand. I believe that eternity's inquisition will spare me, and its sentence will be the same as the one Giordano Bruno received.

"Execute most mercifully. Without drawing blood. Burn alive." Fine.

Chapter 15

A marsh, too, can be beautiful. When the morning sun hovers over the tips of the firs. When gleaming arrows, shot by the bog's revelling spirits, fly down through the puddles into a deep sky. When the grassy hummocks along the edge sway with asthenic daisies, sickly girls who get better in the spring. When shimmering lapwings make you jump on to the windowsill, dangle your legs and whistle. When the locomotive hoots like a child playing hide-and-seek, and the church bells hang right here, on the telegraph posts, ringing invisibly. And their peals fall on to the greening earth, and the earth steams.

Garšva recalled the joy he felt after transforming his parents' night table into an altar. He pushed the little table up to the window, covered it with a clean tablecloth that shimmered with his mother's embroidered lilies and tulips. He found himself a white candle in a clay candlestick. He put on his father's summer coat, draped a linen towel around his neck, the red fringe swaying. And Garšva lit the candle. The pale flame quivered in the sunshine. He spread out his arms and raised his head, like a real priest at a real altar. Christ was right there, invisible, just like the church bells. Several Christs were there. The lapwing feathers, the pealing bells, the locomotive whistle, the daisy hummocks, the pale flame.

Dominus vobiscum, said Garšva.

Et cum spiritu tuo, came the reply.

Gloria, Gloria.

Deo gratias, amen, amen.

Son – Redeemer of the world.

Asperges me, gloria ad Confiteor.

His missal was a fat book called *Advice for Cooks*. He

repeated by heart the Latin words, mysterious and beautiful to him in their foreignness.

Credo gloria,
asperges gloria,
Oh God.
Confiteor gloria,
Et cum spiritu tuo.
Amen.
Dominus vobiscum.
Amen.
Kyrie eleison.
Christe eleison.
Amen.

And when young Garšva couldn't remember any more Latin words, he added his own to the prayer.

Christ, hear us.
Christ, hear our prayers.
Father, God in Heaven,
Holy Spirit,
God.
Credo gloria,
confiteor gloria.
Amen.

Et cum spiritu tuooo..., he sang forth. Young Garšva had run out of prayer. He threw off his father's coat, blew out the candle, wrapped the towel around his neck, raised his head even higher and sang out at the top of his lungs.

The falcon comes soaring, above the green woooo...

*

Palanga. A quiet summer resort. The wide, flat, yellow beach, where the poet Maironis still strolled. The small, crooked pines, distant relatives of the conifers that once dripped yellow sap capturing insects for all time. The motionless Ronžė River. The wooden villas and the smaller houses calling themselves villas. The pebble-strewn paths. The Lourdes of fake caves eternalised by photographers. The Kurhauzas leftover from tsarist times, where dances were held in the evenings, where they picked a king for the season, usually some actor, dance instructor or wrestler. The seaside restaurant, whose steps reached down to the sea, writers, artists, couples and the odd single person lounging at its small tables. Count Tiškevičius's decaying stately palace stands proud in its antiquity, the red roses, and a stone Christ blesses the roses.[95] On a wooden platform in the pine forest, a military brass band plays a medley from *La Traviata*, "In a Persian Market" or especially energetic military marches, all arranged by a red-cheeked, round-bellied conductor who was fond of jokes, women and vodka. The little chapel on Birutė's Hill, the sparse pines on Swedes' Hill.[96] Famous spots familiar in the finest detail, the same every summer but missed and longingly rediscovered by the same holidaymakers summer after summer. And the sun, slicing open a strip of horizon on calm evenings, paints it in blood, just as a calm sunset ought to. And the moon's night-time path to the other side, to that land once inhabited by blonde, bearded Vikings. And the sea's soft moans, and the sea's fierce whispers. And the stars, the same ones, of course, as those seen by embracing lovers. And the sand. On the shore, the dunes, the paths. Shaken out of shoes, brushed off bodies, the dry and damp, yellow and brown sands of Palanga. The million grains that one would like to take back to the city. So as not to forget Palanga, the most peaceful summer resort in Northern Europe. And the pier.[97]

95 A lavish neo-Romantic estate built for the wealthy Lithuanian-Polish Tiškevičius (Tyszkievicz) aristocratic family.

96 A neo-Gothic chapel that was built in 1898 on Birutė's Hill, overlooking the sea. The site, on the grounds of the Tiškevičius estate, was a pagan sanctuary and it is thought that during the fourteenth century the priestess Birutė, mother of Grand Duke Vytautas, lived and was buried there.

97 A long, L-shaped wooden pier jutting out from the beach in the centre of the resort town, the Palanga pier is a popular place to walk and enjoy the scenery.

That summer, the one during which Garšva orated, sang, danced, and stared at the tree, he also swam around the end of the pier. It was the final heat. The L-shaped structure shimmered with multicoloured robes, bathing suits, girls' hair ribbons, rubber caps, sparkling eyes. The sun exploded above all of their heads. There had been a storm the day before, and though the wind had died down, substantial waves still crashed between the eroded posts supporting the pier, broke once, frothing, and then, diminished, rolled diagonally towards the women's beach. Garšva glanced at the open sea. It was painful to look at the glistening foam. The horizon crawled towards Sweden. The first, barely visible waves disappearing in the sky. Garšva wanted to turn around, but then he heard the girls' voices, and was left staring at the spraying waters, at the waves' determination to erode the wooden bridge posts.

"Garšva won't win," said a high-pitched voice.

"He's so thin."

"Yeah," agreed a lower voice.

"Mažeika will win. Garšva will come in second or third."

"I don't think Garšva will be able to handle it – when he gets around the end of the pier and has to battle the waves," the lower voice concluded.

Garšva turned his head. Two blonde girls, tanned and ruthless with their sparkling white teeth, stood nearby. Two tall girls, solid and proud in their awareness of their own bodies. Garšva puffed out his chest and walked by.

"Well, someone's sure of himself!" he heard the lower voice say.

Mažeika was leaning against the railing, waiting. The champion three seasons in a row. A typical swimmer, with a broad chest, lumps of muscle in his arms, legs and back. His brown hair was faded from the sun, and his humped nose, bristly eyebrows, square chin and the black amber in his silver ring all stood out aggressively. The third contender sat on the ground massaging his legs. A handsome, dark-haired young man. Well-proportioned, rounded, his flowing muscles still covered by a layer of childish fat.

"On your marks!" shouted the referee.

The threesome got into position. A shot, and they jumped into the waves. Garšva used the crawl, a stroke his opponents had not yet learned. They were swimming on the side of the open sea, the perpendicular section of the bridge pier lay parallel to the shore. It was possible to swim the crawl. He just had to dive through the occasional wave to avoid being thrown against the posts. Garšva's opponents were swimming breaststroke and, without realising it, he reached the end of the pier, turned around, and started back in the opposite direction. Now the real battle began. The crawl was no longer an option. He had to plough into the waves with his chest as they mercilessly dragged him towards the beach.

Garšva looked up. On the pier, at the rails, stood the spectators, a multicoloured band in the blinding glitter of the sun. Garšva thought that he could see the blonde girls standing nearby, waving their arms. Garšva swam breaststroke, breathing deeply and rhythmically, bowing his head when a wave that had broken through the posts tried to carry him to the shore. He glanced back. Mažeika was getting closer. When Garšva had rounded the end of the pier, Mažeika had been so far away, and now, suddenly, he was approaching. "My arm muscles aren't strong enough," the thought flashed through his mind. Garšva felt fear – the childish kind, and the kind he had felt while looking at the tree. And then he saw the band of spectators break up. A brown body hung in the air. The round boy was being hauled up with a rope. He couldn't make it. Garšva looked back once again. Only Mažeika was left behind him.

Garšva squinted. He ploughed forward, towards his goal, towards the ladder that one climbs to get up on to the pier. He no longer felt his arms, legs or abdomen. Only his head and his heavy, slowing breath. And the longing to lose.

By turning to the right and shouting "Rope, rope!" But Garšva kept swimming. How far was the ladder – that one climbs to get back up on to the pier? It was far away. An eternity away. He felt a sudden stab in his brain. To his left, right alongside him, swam Mažeika. Muscles dove in and out of the water and foam, and Garšva could clearly see the open mouth, the whites of the eyes. While Garšva floated in place, Mažeika swam. Terribly slowly. The head, armpits and ribs crept forward, then the orange trunks, and then the legs, spreading out and back together like scissors. "He's passing me," thought Garšva. He raised his head. The ladder was just ahead. Maybe ten metres away.

Then Garšva took a deep breath and plunged down into the water. The realisation hit him. He does have arms and legs. He scissored rapidly, the water pressing down on him. Then he would breathe out a little and scissor again. The layers of water became even heavier, there was no air left in his lungs, and then Garšva came up. The ladder was in front of him. He grabbed it, but didn't have the strength to climb up. Someone prodded him. Mažeika was hanging there next to him.

"Can't you go up?" he asked.

Garšva wanted to say "No," but he couldn't even do that. There was no air left in the world, and his heart pounded in his chest. Mažeika put his arm around him and they climbed up the ladder together.

Now back up on the wooden boards of the pier, Garšva took several deep breaths. Someone covered him in a robe. The world was nauseously green and Garšva wanted to sleep, to stop existing. His body shook in a delicate quiver. Someone shoved a silver statue of a woman into his hands and said something. And then, only after a few minutes, did he understand that he had won, that he had beaten Mažeika by half a body length.

He walked home with two assistants, a blonde girl on

each arm. And Garšva told them all about the crawl, the newest style of swimming. If the sea had been calmer he would have beaten Mažeika by fifty metres. His bare feet dug into the warm sand of the dunes and he realised that winning is great fun. He put his arms around the girls' shoulders, smiled charmingly, and said:

"Maybe you two would like me to train you?"

"We would, we would!" cried the higher voice.

"We'll meet tomorrow at one on the bridge, okay?" decided the lower voice, taking the statue from Garšva because it was awkward for him to carry it.

"Very good," Garšva agreed, sounding like an old master.

Three blonde heads swimming at Palanga. A peaceful summer resort.

...

There were quiet nights in Kaunas as well, in June, when barely a couple of hours separate dusk from dawn. On one of those nights, having seen Jonė home, Antanas Garšva was walking back along Laisvės alėja. The lights in the shop windows had already gone out. Halos radiated from the boulevard's lanterns, the mature linden trees lit up like women who've put on their make-up. The policemen's colourful uniforms faded, the white-coated sausage sellers rolled their carts and the Soboras dominated the slowly brightening sky. Garšva's shoes clacked on the pavement. Snubbed prostitutes sadly scanned the alleys. Two unlucky drunks climbed up to the Rambynas beer hall only to be shoved back down by a broad-shouldered bouncer. The morning's roses waited in the flower store's dark display window, and the lanterns like an alchemist's hands turned the roses into little glass statues and you could see dead women's faces in their blooms. A distinguished gentleman in a light-coloured suit stood on Mickevičius Street, smoked a cigarette and waited for a bus.

The Soboras drew nearer. In the sky, stars that had barely begun to burn faded. Antanas Garšva did not turn into

Mickevičius Street. He decided to climb up Vytautas Hill to get a view of Kaunas at dawn. He skirted the Soboras. The stone mass flattened itself against the ground. On this unreal night, this sister of the white nights of the North, the Byzantine force, the arcs of Mongolian swords, and the sleepiness of Russian monasteries were a heavy and divided God who saw only conspiracy amongst his subjects. The carpet of Laisvės alėja led up to the Soboras and Kaunas's diminutive buildings carried it gifts as if it were a khan of the Golden Horde recently converted to Christianity. The granite steps, the heavy doors, the columns and cupolas, the cross. A golden cube, where both Moscow and Rome prayed.

Antanas Garšva walked along the boulevard and came to Vytautas Hill – dark and fragrant with summer. Flashes of empty benches. Neighbouring rows of two-storey houses. Beyond the promenade, the avenue became a street from a posh summer resort. Garšva heard someone crying and didn't immediately understand where the sound was coming from. On such a night it could have been a ghost. Garšva was young and his imagination easily evaded the pincers of reason. High tones, full and rhythmic, cut through the silence at the foot of the hill. An old ghost blew into a willow flute, holding the pauses, and the flute moaned. Garšva stopped. "It's a theme," he thought. "I don't care who is crying. In one of these houses there's an open window, a child has woken up in its crib, but for me it's an old ghost, from the times when a sturdy castle stood where the Nemunas and the Neris meet. The ghost's loved ones have died off. His beloved fairy drowned herself because her golden tresses had become frayed and thin. The field god hung himself in the castle ruins because they took away his fields, and he had so loved this fertile triangle. A brave and cruel grand duke's soul strangled himself with a silk scarf, his steel armour melted, and he could no longer burn crusaders' souls at the stake. And the spirit of the grand duke's daughter, the one so beloved by one of Šarūnas's warriors, went mad. She wandered down to Raudonė Castle, wrapped herself in a white shroud, and walked through the linden tree park singing the same song.

> *Vai žydėk, žydėk,*
> *Balta obelėle –*
> *Vai žydėk, žydėk,*
> *Sausa be lapelių!*
> *Vai kaip man žydėt,*
> *Baltai obelėlei, –*
> *Vai kaip man žydėt,*
> *Sausai be lapelių?* [98]

The cry came from nearby. Antanas Garšva glanced at the last bench on the Avenue. Something white lay there. It was a baby. The manikin was wrapped in a dirty cotton apron. The yellowish face wrinkled in the starlight. "Clever trick, to leave the child in a rich neighbourhood." Garšva took the baby in his arms. In the coolness of the dawn Garšva felt his arms warming up. The foundling stopped crying. "He must have been nursed recently, was just missing his mother's warmth. But what do I do with him? Could he be a gift from an old ghost? Don't be silly. This is serious." Garšva remembered that there was a police station nearby, on Gediminas Street. He went back in that direction, carefully holding the now calmly breathing manikin. "I'll have one of these when I marry Jonė. When I'm a famous poet and receive a national award. He'll stop crying when

---

98 Lithuania folk song:
Bloom, oh bloom,
My white apple tree –
Bloom, oh bloom,
Yet dry without leaves!
> *And how am I to bloom,*
> *A white apple tree, –*
> *And how am I to bloom,*
> *Yet dry without leaves?*

I pick him up. That's not bourgeois. It's mystical. It took a long time for the earth, the grass, the dinosaurs and Laisvės alėja to take shape. It's inexplicable and true. I'll love Jonė, and I'll hear cries and I'll hear laughter. I'll see my child's face, full of wisdom. Wise, because he doesn't yet know anything. A little bubble who'll inspire optimistic poems. I might even be original, and become famous. To become famous these days you have to write optimistic poems."

Antanas Garšva walked into the police station. The policeman on duty was writing something.

"I found this," said Garšva, holding the little person right in front of his face, as though he were a cracked porcelain vase. "On a bench, near Vytautas Hill."

"What the hell!" exclaimed the policeman. "That's the second one tonight. Another Jewish girl in trouble from some soldier. Put him over there, on the table. We'll fill out a report."

By the time Antanas Garšva returned to the street, day was breaking. He chose the most direct route home. He climbed up Aušra Lane.[99] Kaunas lay below. The cathedral rose above the bluish dusk. He saw the chimneys of the Tilmans textile mill, the bends of the Nemunas, the Linksmadvaris embankment, the sky's pink rebirth. Rotting leaves crackled. White plastered cottages poked out of the trees, the day continued to brighten. Garšva paused at the top of Aušra Lane. He leaned against the wobbly railing and said to himself, "I want to marry Jonė. I want a child. I want poems. I want money. I want honour. I want to be happy. I want to live," as though he'd released a golden fish from his net and it had decided to fulfil his wishes instantly.

---

99   Aušra: dawn (Lithuanian).

CONCLUSION

Antanas Garšva opens the door and lets out a girl in a painfully red dress, and then he sees Elena. She's wearing the familiar grey suit, the veil from her grey beret is lowered over her face, and her stockings have been put on properly. She's speaking with O'Casey.

"Elena!" shouts Garšva. They hear him and come towards the elevator. O'Casey asks, smiling:

"Not too many passengers, eh, Tony?"

"Not too many," Garšva replies moving his lips but barely making a sound.

"I'm taking number nine out temporarily. Take number seven and have a talk. I'll give you a shout when there's work."

"Thank you, O'Casey," whispers Garšva.

"Thank you, Mister O'Casey," says Elena.

"Always at your service, madam," and he opens number seven.

"But just in case – keep riding, Tony. You know, if the manager…"

"I understand. Thanks."

Garšva gives the handle a push, and they start going up.

"It's a nice elevator," says Elena.

"Yes. Because it's a nice hotel."

"My ears are ringing a bit."

"They're fast elevators," says Garšva, and stops the elevator on the seventeenth floor. He doesn't open the door. He looks at Elena.

"You came. That's good. You came. Lift up the veil."

And Elena lifts up the veil, and it lies back on the top of the beret. Garšva stares at the familiar face.

"You came," he repeats.

They don't move.

"Why didn't you let me in?" asks Elena. Garšva is still looking at the beloved face. The same eyes, curve of the lips, the same lipstick, layer of light powder. Standing under the light of the matt bulb she looks as though she has just returned from a lost world. A Baldovinetti Madonna. Time has turned around, the past is coming back. He no longer has to listen to the fists pounding on the closed door. The steps in the stairwell fade, a small grey woman walks along the street and disappears around the bend. The past is still coming back. Garšva puts his left arm around Elena, pulls her close and kisses her on the lips. Slowly, softly, like a mother. A miracle has occurred. And the miracle is gentle, like Elena's lips, her face, her body, her breath. And at the same time, without looking at the control board, Garšva switches the buttons. They descend and stop on the twelfth.

"Forgive me," says Garšva. "I didn't let you in. You can imagine what I felt when I didn't let you in. And you know why. I was afraid of my illness. Forgive me. I love you. So much. I overdid it, Elena. But now I'm sure. I'll get better. I really believe I'll get better. And I'll be with you. I know that I deceived your husband, I'll speak to him again. Definitively. And you'll be mine, I believe that you'll be mine, if you came here, to the elevator."

"I'll be yours," says Elena, and they rise again. To the seventeenth.

"When we meet next I'll tell you everything. Too many thoughts. Too many shards. Too little happiness."

The small grey woman and uniform number 87. The bare, polished walls of the elevator shine. The past is still coming back. All the women come back. All in one.

"You can't imagine how worried I was. You're ill, you don't love me, you were taken to the hospital, you were hit by a car, you found another woman."

"Please, come back, come back to my room," says Garšva

and presses the handle. They swoop downward and stop on the sixth.

"Tomorrow I'll go to the doctor. The day after tomorrow I'm off work. Come the day after tomorrow. Early. I can't wait to see you again. You have no idea how happy I am. The day after tomorrow we'll drink – oh no, don't worry, just a little, and we'll make love a lot. And, if it isn't enough for us, I'll get a few days off. And... I think, I'm sorry, you have to go now. O'Casey's a good starter, but I don't want to abuse his kindness. It's the second time he's helping me out today."

When they arrive at the bottom, Elena asks:

"You haven't been to the doctor?"

"Once. And I didn't go back a second time, even though he insisted I must."

"See him tomorrow. Alright?"

"Like I said, I'll go to the doctor's," and Garšva opens the door.

O'Casey approaches and Elena reaches out her hand.

"I know that in America it isn't customary to shake hands to say goodbye. But I am very grateful to you. Today..." she doesn't finish and smiles. O'Casey takes her hand and kisses it.

"I'm Irish, madam, so I respect European customs. I wish you all the best," and O'Casey withdraws discreetly.

"You're stunning today," says Garšva. "And your stockings are on straight."

"I was thinking about you. Goodbye. I'll see you the day after tomorrow."

"Goodbye."

And Elena walks away. Down the dark red carpet. Exquisite in her fine proportions, as though she had been created by a female god. She disappears beyond the corner, and she's gone.

O'Casey comes up and asks, "Who is she?"

"My fiancée."

"Nice woman. And very attractive."

"Thanks, O'Casey."

And O'Casey claps Garšva on the shoulder.

"Go back to number nine, Tony. And wipe your lips. She gave you some colour."

Number nine rises, number nine falls. The express from the ninth to the eighteenth. Your floor, here we are, thank you, the button, thank you, here we are. The green arrow lights up, Antanas Garšva reaches out a white-gloved hand, that's it, we're going up. Hand on handle. And the floors twinkle above his head. 1, 2, 3, 4, 5, 6, 7, 8, 9, 10, 11.

A splendid up *ir* down. This is how the departed fly around in the afterlife. Children's kites, summer butterflies, planets, dandelion fluff. This is how a fairy tale flies, that most serious kind of nonsense, unique to humans.

Here we are, thank you, a guest exits, hand to handle, we're going up, someone stopped the elevator, the door opens, a guest enters, we're going up. Going up, going up. The eighteenth, here we are. Everyone exits.

The bare, polished elevator walls glisten. Adam and Eve have returned to Paradise. But there are no fantastic flowers or docile panthers, no ambiguous serpent. Between the plastic walls, under the light of the matt bulb and the floor numbers, the first two humans stand, embracing.

We wait for a red square and a green arrow. And we go down. Going down, going down. The same ritual. Up *ir* down, up *ir* down.

I'm an elevator angel in a uniform from an operetta. Those kinds of angels tend to be cheery. They have pink bottoms. They'll even dare to tug at God's coat-tails, while He is busy with the tragic problems of the universe. And God smiles benevolently. "Hey, you kids, off you go to the Holy Virgin – she'll give you a cookie in My Name." And the angels fly in a group, pinching each other, filling Heaven with a great racket, so that even Saint Thomas Aquinas raises his head from the letter he is writing to

Jacques Maritain, explaining that the God of the Exodus is not a being but He is Being itself – as every being can either exist or not exist.

I'm a transplanted acacia bush. My roots draw the new earth's sap, and, though some of my branches have wilted, my crown is verdant, and a graceful bird has landed on my viscous leaves. It lifts its grey-stockinged feet up and down and cheerfully screeches a song.

> Oh, Susan Van Dusan,
> The goal of my choosin'
> She sticks to my bosom
> Like glue...

I'm an experienced hermit sick and tired of the desert, the sackcloth, the cane, meditation and my mossy lair. I'm a hermit who travels to the big city and then remembers that there are still gold coins buried in his basement, and chats up a young girl.

I'm a Lithuanian *kaukas* who has found himself a female companion. And we'll find ourselves a master who'll give us some new linen pants for all the jobs we do.

I'm manikin number 87 in eight-million-strong New York.

I'm happy.

...

Five past one. Garšva leaves the hotel. It's a warm night. The advertising lights have gone out. His shoes clack on the pavement, like they did in Kaunas. The same freshness, the same stars, occasional passers-by. Kaunas has stretched up to the clouds. The skyscraper towers sway, the marshy town's church bells have gone silent, the old ghost has slipped his willow flute under his coat and gone off to sleep somewhere on 3rd Avenue. The becalmed ocean no longer murmurs. The tugboats and ships have nestled against the coast. Sailors sleep embracing their cheap girlfriends. Tomorrow two blonde girls will jump into the blue Baltic. The glass windows of Gimbels department store are dark.

Stairs, stairs, stairs. The mannequins sleep standing, like horses, and the subway echoes. A drunk sways by the door to the Men's, talking to himself. "I'm clever. Tomorrow I'll show him, that son-of-a-bitch!" The subway's night crew, cleaning women and young men going home after their dates, are waiting on the platform, as is Antanas Garšva. The noise intensifies and the train careers from around the corner. Two green eyes, two red ones, a white window. Brakes screech, doors open. Beyond them – wicker benches, sleepy faces, returning home. Home. BMT Broadway Line. Tomorrow. The day after tomorrow. Tomorrow and the day after tomorrow – magical words.

Antanas Garšva gets up at nine. He shaves, washes, eats two eggs, drinks a cup of coffee. Then goes out to the store and calls Doctor Ignas.

"Hello. I'd like to see you."

"It's about time. How are you feeling?" replies Doctor Ignas reproachfully.

"Terrific. Yesterday everything turned upside down. Oh, forgive me. Everything turned right side up. Nevertheless, I'd like to see you."

"If you're feeling alright, come at around two. Right now I have to visit some patients."

"Great. I'll be there at two. After that I'll head to work. See you later."

"See you."

Garšva goes back home. He sits down at the table. He finds a sheet of paper. Picks up a pen.

It's cosy in Garšva's room this morning. A sunbeam has slipped through the window and illuminated the Chagall woman's cloudy hair. Book dust rises and blends with cigarette smoke. The clear blue colour of the room. The chair creaks, the pen scratches. The writer's rhythmic breath.

True peace has finally come to me. I'm objective, I'm a medium, I don't need to be absolutely original. My soul has found a relationship with the world. I'll be unknown, like an ancient Chinese painter. I'll follow in the footsteps of the great masters. And I'll thank my God for those forgotten pieces of my life: the time I played at being a priest giving mass, the race, the foundling. I'm thankful for the young Russian. When I prayed, swam, dreamt of a child, killed a man, I was sure. I was a synthesis of body and soul. I am Jin Shengtan, who, on a clear morning after a long rain, once again hears the birds' voices, draws open the curtains and sees the freshly bathed sun shining over the forest.

My responses have welded together my life, my observations, my ruminations. A few little grains. A few poems. A single, tangible truth.

I forgot that I have only one life to live. I have been living as though I were preparing for yet other lives. And I lost a great deal of time. Though, like some American said – "Life begins at forty." A man only takes shape at forty, the Romans argued. I'm forty, and now I'll start to live. And when death comes, I will greet it calmly: *Ave Caesar, vivans te salutat!*[100]

Lioj, ridij, augo, lepo, leputeli – trills the nightingale. A boggy marsh. Fairies whir through the air. Toads watch the universe through bulging eyes. Triangular firs, the towers of Lithuanian shrines rise to the stars. To be born, to live, to die. To climb up on to high benches. Two shabby *kaukai* accompany Christ. "Give us some new pants, turn the marsh waters to red wine." In the honeycombs, the ears of wheat, the rue and the lilies, the embraces of gnarled trunks, the tangled roots, the flowing waters – You are to be found.

Lioj. Ridij, Augo.

I have understood myself. The shards fit together. A child observing a landscape. Road, stream, hills, deer. A serpent hugging the ground. Fairies combing their tresses. The

100 See note 91, but there's a small change: the translation here is "Hail Caesar, a living person [singular] salutes you!"

gliding mist. Day darkens, brightness darkens. Lapwing feathers, tolling bells, *dominus vobiscum.*

Antanas Garšva lights himself yet another cigarette. He feels a pain at the top of his head. "I've smoked too much," he tells himself. Garšva crushes the cigarette in an ashtray. He twirls his pen ambivalently. The pain is bearable. It will go away. Like the grim past. Two o'clock – Doctor Ignas. Tomorrow – Elena? The day after? The day after tomorrow I'll ask for time off. And, very possibly, I'll switch hotels. Everything will be renewed. Love, poetry, people, streets.

There will be no more need for Hear me, My Elevator. Hear me, my Childhood. Hear me, my Death, *credo gloria* or *confiteor gloria.* There will be no more need for Hear me – my Sin, my Madness. Day darkens, brightness darkens. A choir of *kaukai,* field and harvest gods. *Lioj.*

I'll make it in time. I promise. I will give you. A carnelian ring. A wagon in Queens Plaza. My love.

...

Elena is taking a bath. White foam slides down her legs and explodes into iridescent bubbles. "He will kiss my legs. Slowly. When he kisses my wrists, I'll believe my happiness. I won't torment him. I'll restrain myself."

She gets up, a grey Aphrodite in a cast-iron tub, turns on the shower, and warm spurts of water wash off the foam.

"I'll ring the bell and the door will open. Faster than I can pull back my fingers. Tomorrow."

...

The pain is annoying. The top of the head burns. There is no fear. But the peace is fading too. Pain and indifference. Sudden stabs, and then a deaf, rolling ball. The ball is growing and will soon escape. The pen has stopped scratching. I'm out of pills. Garšva gets up, goes to the kitchen and returns with a glass. He drinks some White Horse. Sits down again, and again picks up the pen.

The white woman plays. *O felix culpa quae talem et tantum*

meruit habere redemptorem.[101] Two *vėlės* and a harpsichord. The gilded statues run up the granite steps. The torches in their hands have gone out. And the sculptural noblemen's heads rejoice. *Ė, ridij, augo! Ė, felix culpa!* I love the blue veins on your legs. Your damp eyelashes. Tristan and Isolde's sword, the mole on your neck. *Lioj.*

Amber insects creep along the sand. Towards the blue Baltic. "*Vai žydėk, žydėk, balta obelėle,*" sings the *vėlė*, wrapped in a white shroud. *O felix culpa!* My childhood, my life, my death. *Lioj.*

No pain. But the ball is enormous. It no longer fits inside the brain, and yet it cannot escape through the skull. A thought struggles to be heard: "Must see Doctor Ignas." Garšva hurriedly puts on his suit. His fingers don't cooperate. The pant zipper chokes but he manages to get it free. A tie? Never mind. Money? There are eight dollars on the table. Enough for a taxi.

The brown man in the elevator. I just remembered him. Is he Death? A warning from God?

God, You see how miserable I am.

I know I'm too late, but save me.

I promise.

I'll tear up my notes, my poems.

I won't think in ways that offend You.

I'll pray.

I'll enter a monastery.

God, though I am dying, help me.

I believe that You can forgive at the very last minute.

An entire life.

God, oh God, I offer myself into Your hands...

Oh no, I am a manikin, a manikin, oh God.

Oh Gooood!...

"*Zoori, zoori,*" whispers Garšva.

Where is *zoori*? What is *zoori*? Why is *zoori*? I've lost *zoori*. Help me find it! Could it have flown away? Help

101 See note 34.

me! Antanas Garšva whimpers. He screams. He pounds the walls with his fists. The pins pop out. The Chagall reproduction flips around and hangs backwards.

...

Stanley is walking along the bridge. He is weaving slightly. Having thrown the Seagram's bottle into the East River. He finishes a cigarette, tosses it, and looks around. The bridge is empty. At the very end a man recedes. Stanley leans against the railing and stares at Greater New York. Rocks built on rocks. Skyscrapers. Ships and tugboats float by. Chimneys stick out in the distance. A train thunders on to the bridge, shaking the tracks. The clamour approaching fast.

Carefully, Stanley lifts his legs over the railing. He doesn't look at the water. "*Idz srač*," he says, and falls silently down.

...

A few minutes to twelve. Garšva sits on the flowered linoleum. In paradise. By the blue hills. Surrounded by blooming flowers and giant butterflies lazily fanning their wings. Garšva feels cool, he feels good. There is a rose in his hand. A dead woman's face. Its petals as soft as curtains. Garšva holds a sheaf of papers that he is tearing into thin strips. His face is happy. A peaceful idiot's. He smells the paper. A chinchilla's face.

...

The book dust continues to float upward. A sunbeam lights up a bare wall, the reproduction now hangs in shadow. Clear blue. Cosy.

THE END

1952–1954

Translator's Note

Any literary translation can be seen as an inherently impossible exercise, but a text that itself plays with translation and with the émigré's movement back and forth between languages, and does so in multiple voices, presents particular challenges. Antanas Škėma's *Balta drobulė* brilliantly conveys the displaced person's constant feeling of dislocation and cultural adjustment by mixing fragments of English and other European languages into the speech and thoughts of the main characters. This English version of Škėma's novel attempts to preserve some of that linguistic richness by leaving several key words, as well as passages of folksong, in Lithuanian within the main body of the text, with translations and explanations provided in footnotes; the decision to leave the phrase "up *ir* down" as it appeared in the original was made to convey some of the blended flavour of the text, as other instances of émigré language and slang were inevitably lost in translation (e.g., "labsteriai" simply became "lobsters"). It is hoped that the end result is in the spirit of Škėma's faith in the possibility of a synthesis between Lithuanian and other languages and cultures, and in the possibilities offered by that synthesis. This translation would not have been possible without the participation of leading Škėma scholar Loreta Mačianskaitė who provided unflagging support from the beginning of the project, Baltic Studies scholar Violeta Kelertas who read an early version of the draft, and Jurgis Vaitkūnas without whom the whole up *ir* down would not have been nearly as meaningful.

A personal recollection from Jonas Mekas, American avant-garde filmmaker of Lithuanian origin

I think it was in 1947, in the Kassel Displaced Persons camp, that myself with a couple of younger, post-Škėma generation writers, we read one of the short stories that had just came out in Škėma's first collection of prose pieces. We were taken by one of his short stories which ended with a very clinical description of a spittoon by hospital patient's bed. It was so minimal and so clinical like nothing before in Lithuanian literature. As much as we were critical of the writings of the generation "before us," we admitted that Antanas Škėma was "OK."

I have to add, that our small group who considered ourselves a "new" generation of Lithuanian literature, we were only some ten years younger...

Later, some five years later, in Brooklyn, I met Škėma in person. He had just opened a theatre studio. I decided to join it. I have to confess that my joining his studio was not motivated by my wanting to become an actor: I joined it because I was falling in love with a young woman who had joined it... And it was amazing to find out how Škėma was able to take a sentence from a play and analyse it in the same clinical, down to earth way as he did with the spittoon in his short story. Piece by piece he was bringing the sentence alive in front of our eyes, very factually and clinically. Only later I found out that before joining Kaunas and later Vilnius National Lithuanian Theatre, where he worked as an actor and director, he had studied medicine and law. So now he applied it all to his writing. No baloney, as they say. No

192

unnecessary ornamentation. Algimantas Mockus, a poet of "our" ("younger") generation later described his generation as a "generation without ornamentation." Škėma, more than any other Lithuanian writer of the immediate post-war period, with BALTA DROBULĖ represents most uniquely that generation, the generation with no ornamentation.

New York, November 2016